PUFFIN BOOKS

BROTHER WULF
THE LAST SPOOK

Also available by Joseph Delaney

BROTHER WULF
THE LAST SPOOK

JOSEPH DELANEY

PUFFIN

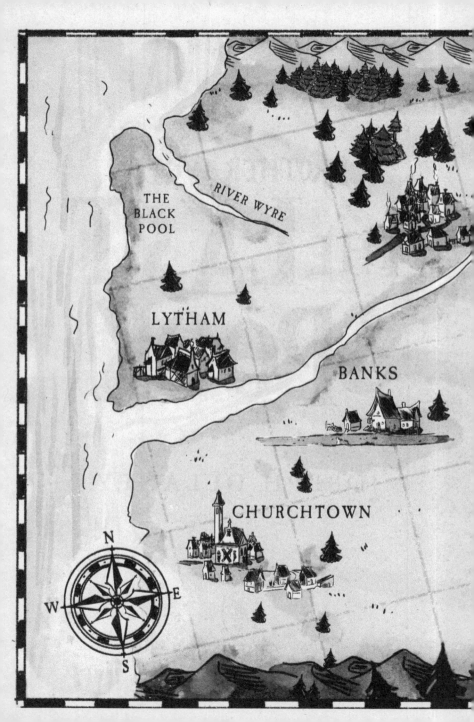

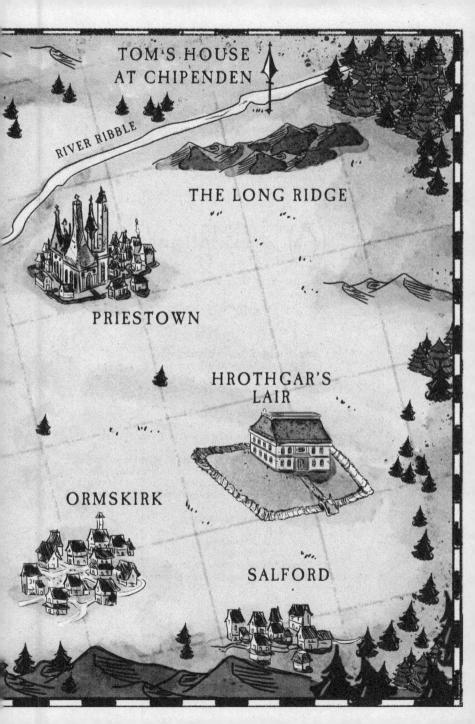

PUFFIN BOOKS

UK | USA | Canada | Ireland | Australia
India | New Zealand | South Africa

Puffin Books is part of the Penguin Random House group of companies
whose addresses can be found at global.penguinrandomhouse.com.

www.penguin.co.uk
www.puffin.co.uk
www.ladybird.co.uk

First published 2022

001

Text copyright © Joseph Delaney, 2022
Map illustration by Alessia Trunfio

The moral right of the author has been asserted

Set in 10/16.5 pt Palatino LT Std
Typeset by Jouve (UK), Milton Keynes
Printed and bound in Great Britain by Clays Ltd, Elcograf S.p.A.

The authorized representative in the EEA is Penguin Random House Ireland,
Morrison Chambers, 32 Nassau Street, Dublin DO2 YH68

A CIP catalogue record for this book is available from the British Library

ISBN: 978–0–241–56845–3

All correspondence to:
Puffin Books
Penguin Random House Children's
One Embassy Gardens, 8 Viaduct Gardens, London SW11 7BW

MIX
Paper from
responsible sources
FSC
www.fsc.org   FSC® C018179

Penguin Random House is committed to a
sustainable future for our business, our readers
and our planet. This book is made from Forest
Stewardship Council® certified paper.

For Marie

ALICE'S TALE

1

THE POMPOUS BISHOP

The pompous bishop was beginning to annoy me.

Truth is, it ain't hard to do that now. My patience has all but gone, blown into tatters by time and sorrow. A long life I've had and not all of it's been good. I was born into the Pendle clans and my mother was a witch called Bony Lizzie.

Being raised by witches ain't the ideal start in life.

But my name is Alice Deane and I just had to make the best of it. I certainly did that. Once I was the most powerful witch in the County. But those days are long gone.

I was sitting near the door, right at the back of the chapel. My head was bowed low and my face was shadowed by my hood. There were a few people scattered around me, most of them kneeling and praying – one or two even older than I was.

The bishop was seated in a high chair with his back to the altar. And the arrogant look on his face showed that he was full of self-importance.

I watched him settle into his chair, wriggling on the straight-backed wooden seat. He looked as comfortable as a frog sizzling in a greasy frying pan. But it wasn't the heat he'd be feeling. It was late autumn and the chapel was plagued with cold draughts. No doubt they were blowing up his cassock and freezing his bum. That thought made me smile.

It was the first time that I'd smiled for quite some time.

The bishop was here to deal with petitioners. It was his duty. Once a week, he travelled to a different church and listened to his flock. The sour look on his face told me that he didn't like it. He couldn't wait to ride back to Kersal Abbey and tuck into a big venison supper before crawling into his warm bed.

I'd been there for almost an hour and a dozen or so people had begged him for help. Each time, the bishop had given the same response:

'We will pray for you.'

There was a big problem to be solved, a great danger. All of the petitions had related to it in some way. But prayer wouldn't solve this.

That was why I was here.

Suddenly the chapel door was thrust open. Swollen by the rain, it grated on the damp flags. Two people entered. The first was a monk – a stranger to me – who pushed it shut after them to keep out the draughts. Then, skeletal in his flapping cassock, he strode up the aisle towards the bishop. Behind him was a very tall young red-cheeked farmer trying to keep up.

They halted directly before the bishop and the farmer opened his mouth to speak but was silenced by a gesture from the thin monk who spoke for him.

'This is John Ashton of Glover's Farm. He has young children, my lord, and the demon has claimed all three of them, demanding that they should be delivered to the dark tower by midnight. They are being escorted there even as we speak. John Ashton begs for you to intercede.'

That made me nervous. If that was true, we didn't have much time.

I watched the bishop close his eyes and steeple his hands as if in prayer. It was what he'd done when facing each previous petitioner.

The farmer's children would be dragged to the dark tower by some of the locals who would be only too eager to do so. After all, it was in their own interests. If the command wasn't obeyed, the angry so-called demon would lay waste to the nearby villages and farms the following night. There would be lots of deaths.

Of course, it wasn't a demon. That was just priest talk. The creature was something else from the dark, but it was just as dangerous.

Farmer Ashton was now kneeling, head bowed, awaiting the bishop's reply.

'We shall pray for you, my son,' the bishop said at last. 'The whole abbey will pray. If God is willing our prayers will be answered.'

Despite all the wealth of the Church and its armed servants – a group of whom had accompanied the bishop – it was impossible for the bishop to do anything to help directly. I knew that unless something *was* done it was only a matter of time before the abbey itself would have to be abandoned. Salford was becoming far too dangerous a place for monks. The creature was all-powerful and terrorized the area. When it took a fancy to something or someone it was better to keep out of the way.

It was an eater of human flesh and its appetite was growing – especially for young tender victims.

The farmer remained upon his knees and began to sob, knowing that he had been denied the help he hoped for. The poor man thought that his children were as good as dead.

But he didn't know about me. He didn't know that Alice Deane was sitting in the chapel not too far behind him. He didn't know that things were about to change and that Salford was soon to be a far different place. At least, that's what I was hoping for.

At that moment there was a disturbance, a sudden loud rapping on the door of the chapel.

The bishop nodded to the monk, who walked the length of the aisle, twisted the circular iron handle and dragged the heavy door open once more.

An old man stepped forward into the chapel. He was carrying a staff and a large leather bag and wearing a long cloak with a hood which was not unlike the habit of a monk. He put down the bag at his feet and pulled back the hood to reveal a gaunt face and a white beard with unkempt grey hair.

My heart lurched with anguish.

It was Tom Ward.

Tom was a spook. He dealt with boggarts, ghosts, ghasts and witches – his job was to fight the dark and keep the County safe. Truth was he hadn't been doing much fighting for quite some time. Just keeping breathing had been hard enough.

Time was short so Tom had sent me on ahead while he struggled to complete the journey. His face was lined and weathered by years of exposure to the elements and his back seemed stooped, his body thin and frail, ravaged by age. But the eyes were still young somehow and his keen gaze flickered over the chapel, finally coming to rest upon the bishop.

But rather than move nearer to the altar, he remained by the chapel door. Then he tried to speak, but when he opened his mouth he started to cough. Each cough was a torment for me and I could hardly bear to listen. It went on for a long time until the bishop became impatient and started tapping his knee. At last, Tom managed to get the words out.

'I believe there's a serious local problem – a threat from the dark that should have been dealt with long ago. I've come to help.'

The pompous bishop shook his head in annoyance. 'Go home, old man. Our prayers will do what is necessary.'

Now it was Tom's turn to shake his head. 'Prayers will not suffice here. This is spook's business!' he declared, his voice suddenly surprisingly strong.

Anger reddened the bishop's face and he struggled to his feet before making his reply. His tone of voice suggested that he was talking to a piece of dirt rather than to my Tom.

'Twenty years ago, Spook, I would have had you seized and imprisoned!' he announced, his double chin wobbling with every word. 'Then after a no-doubt short trial you would have been burned at the stake for meddling with the dark and usurping the rightful role of a priest. But now we are entering a new age of darkness. Hell has grown in power and now its denizens stalk the land and neither priest nor spook can do much about them. Only continual prayer and the grace of God can save us! So go home now while you are still able.'

There was a lot of truth in what the bishop had just said. The dark was certainly a lot more powerful. Some even believed that the Fiend, whom priests called the Devil, was returning to rule over it again.

Such a thing sounded impossible. After all, many years earlier Tom had played a big part in his destruction. But a god or goddess could never be totally obliterated. If there was still belief in them, they slowly returned to power. The return of the Fiend was unlikely – but not impossible.

There had been ominous signs of his return. The first warning of that threat had come from a dead witch, Grimalkin. Once she had been the witch assassin of the Malkin clan but had been slain by Golgoth, the Lord of Winter, one of the Old Gods. But Grimalkin was strong and had gathered enough power to make occasional visits to the earth during the hours of darkness. She was able to do this of her own volition, not needing to be summoned by a coven.

She had helped me and Tom many times, but since her warning about the return of the Fiend I'd had no more contact with her. Try as I might she never answered my call and now I feared that the Fiend had destroyed her. After all, she had been one of his most formidable enemies and had done him great hurt in the past.

Tom Ward did not move. Neither did he reply. I knew that he would still be recovering his breath after the long journey from Chipenden. So I left my pew and walked towards him. As I walked, my shoes clicked loudly upon the flags. I liked that sound. It reminded me of just who I was. I took up my usual position, very close to his left-hand side.

I smiled at Tom and he returned my smile.

Then I settled my gaze upon the pompous bishop and I pushed back my hood so that he could take a good gander at my face. Now I was no longer smiling. He tried to hold my gaze but was forced to drop his eyes.

I reached out with my magic and all the candles in the chapel flickered together and then went out, plunging us into darkness.

To do that was easy-peasy. But for anyone else but Tom it would have been the scariest thing they'd seen for many a long year. Already there were screams and moans of fear from nearby. So I didn't leave them in darkness for very long. I reached out again and the candles began to ignite, one by one. As each wick burst into flame, it hissed like a feral cat.

As I told you, my name is Alice Deane. Remember that. Remember it well.

Nobody walks over me or Tom.

Not while I've one gasp of breath left in my body.

'I don't like priests!' I cried out, filling the chapel with my voice. 'And I especially dislike stupid bishops who think themselves more important than they are. But we ain't here to deal with you! We wish to talk to this young man here, the father of the three children that have been claimed.'

Next, I linked arms with Tom and gave him a little of my strength. Immediately, there was a change in him. His back straightened and his face became more animated. Now he looked wiry rather than thin and frail. He appeared to be ten years younger at least.

'Farmer Ashton!' called the Spook, his strong voice echoing back from the chapel walls. 'If you wish to help your children, follow us . . .'

Then Tom turned, pulled open the door and both of us walked out into the darkness. Then, before the bishop could forbid it, the young farmer came to his feet, ran the length of the chapel and dashed out after us.

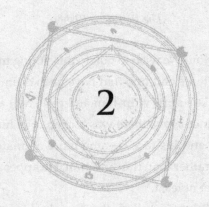

2

BE QUICK OR BE DEAD!

Outside, the air was chilly and it was very dark, the stars and moon obscured by clouds. But darkness don't bother me. I can see better than a sharp-clawed cat.

Tom Ward was already moving north, with me close to his side. I looked over towards the bishop's gang of monks and mercenaries who were waiting beside the chapel. There were at least twenty of them, all heavily armed. Hardly gave me a glance, they did.

Once, many years ago, they might have whistled or made rude remarks because I was young and pretty then. But now my hair is white and although my back is straight and I walk tall and proud, my body is scrawnier than it was. The old are invisible to the young, not worth a glance.

That's one of the biggest mistakes that humans ever make. Creatures of the dark make it too. It's useful to be underestimated. Sometimes you've won even before trouble begins. And sometimes it's good to be invisible. It saves me draining my magic.

Then I heard the farmer running after us. We came to a halt, allowing him to catch up.

'You wanted to speak to me? Well, here I am. Can you help? Can you *really* help us?' asked the farmer anxiously. He was talking to the Spook, not to me. 'My wife's nearly out of her mind and our poor children never did any harm to anybody. Why us? Why did that demon pick upon my family?'

The so-called demon ate human flesh with a preference for young prey and that family had been chosen because of the tender age of the children. But Tom didn't comment. I knew what he was thinking. He saw no need to further upset the young man.

'It isn't a demon,' explained the Spook. 'It's what we call an abhuman – but this one is far more dangerous than most of its kind. Its mother was a witch, so in addition to its savagery and strength it's inherited her gift of dark magic to an unusually powerful degree. I want to speak to you regarding what's about to happen. The best way forward is to free your children before they are imprisoned within the tower. If we manage that, you can take them home to their mother and we'll deal with the abhuman. So follow us and we'll see what we can do.'

Then, without waiting for a reply, Tom set off. I could see that he was forcing himself forward despite his aching bones and his rapid breathing. After a while, the pain must have lessened because he settled into the brisk loping stride of the much younger man he had once been. He'd protected the County for more years than I cared to remember. But this task would be harder than most.

An abhuman with such powerful dark magic at its disposal was a very dangerous opponent. We'd known about the problem, and should have visited Salford much earlier, but Tom had been seriously ill, and had almost died. It had taken all of my skill with magic and herbs to save him. For two months he'd lain very close to death, every breath threatening to be his last. And now, only days after leaving his sickbed, he'd made the exhausting journey here to the outskirts of Salford.

We heard the crying of a child first, immediately followed by gruff reprimands.

'Stop your snivelling! Shut up or you'll feel my boot harder next time!' snarled a deep male voice.

Then the moon briefly came out from behind a bank of clouds, bathing everything in its silver light. For a moment, everyone could see what was happening.

There were five men ahead of us. Two were carrying young children who were perhaps no more than three or four years old. The children had long hair and looked to be the farmer's daughters. The eldest, a boy of about six or seven years old, was being driven before the largest of the men, who was kicking him up the backside every five or six steps.

I sensed Tom bridle with anger at that cruelty and he gripped his staff tighter. But he would leave this to me. The abhuman he would make his business – unless I could talk him out of it. Tom wasn't ready yet for such a strong opponent.

Suddenly Farmer Ashton, who'd been walking several paces to our rear, became aware of what was happening and ran forward. But, as he passed by, I caught him by the elbow and brought him to a halt. He was an exceptionally tall man and I had to stand on my tiptoes to whisper into his ear.

The spell worked quickly and his anger and anguish melted away. He nodded to me then dropped back to walk behind us again. I glanced further ahead. The sky was becoming lighter. Soon the moon would burst free of the clouds. We were approaching a thicket of trees and beyond it, silhouetted against the sky, was the tall tower of black stone which was the lair of the abhuman.

I began to mutter another spell, preparing the way for the confrontation. Despite the cruelty of the kicking these were not evil men. They were just afraid, and desperate to save their own families.

Whether it was the magic in the air or the faint noises of pursuit that alerted them, suddenly the men became aware that they were being followed. They came to a halt and turned to face back towards us.

'Let the children go and return to your homes!' called out Tom. 'We'll deal with the creature in the tower.'

The leader, the big beefy bully of a man who had been kicking the boy, let out a loud raucous laugh and, raising his arm, pointed his forefinger directly at Tom. The other men grinned and the children being carried were placed upon the ground before them as the men paused to watch what promised to be fun.

'Heaven be praised! We're saved at last!' the big man mocked. Then his tone became more ugly and more aggressive. 'All I see is a spook, withered and aged, hardly strong enough to put one foot in front of the other! Those are bold words, old man, but we have our own families to worry about. It's either these children or our own will perish. What chance have you when the bishop and all his men can do nought to help?'

Before Tom could reply, I stepped to his side and shouted seven words right into their faces. It was the spell that I had already prepared.

'*Be gone! Be quick or be dead!*' I cried.

I remembered the words well. It was the same spell I'd uttered all those years ago in Chipenden, when I'd driven away a bunch of boys who had been bullying Tom. He'd been just a young apprentice then, barely thirteen.

And the spell worked again, just as I expected. It was all that was needed.

The five men turned and fled, arms pumping, feet slipping on the damp grass, frantic to be away, their faces contorted with terror.

The farmer stepped towards his children, who ran towards him. He went down on his knees and hugged them. All three of them were weeping. The farmer also had tears dripping from his eyes.

'Thank you! Thank you!' he exclaimed, looking back – this time he was looking at me. This old lady was no longer invisible.

'Ain't no need to thank us,' I said with a smile. 'We'll be on our way now, to do what must be done . . .'

We walked on towards the dark tower, leaving the family behind. Now the real business would begin.

Together we approached the edge of the wood. Tom's left arm, still gripping his staff, now rested across my shoulders; my right arm was round his waist. It felt good to be touching, good to be so close.

'Are you up to this, old man?' I asked. 'You've some way to go before you get your strength back. Perhaps you'd best leave this to me?'

I knew that Tom wouldn't be offended by my use of the word 'old'. We were about the same age – it was a joke shared between us, a term of endearment. Of course, even as a joke Tom would never use that word with me. He once said that I would never be old to him and that, when he gazed into my eyes, I was no different than I had been as the young girl that he had met at Chipenden well over fifty years earlier.

'I'll tell you what,' Tom said. 'You soften the abhuman up – then I'll kill it! And that's the best deal you'll get!'

I smiled at him. 'Ain't anything there that I object to,' I said softly, giving his waist a squeeze.

3

THE BEST SPITTER IN PENDLE

As we walked through the trees, I gathered my power.

There was precious little of it, but I hoped it would suffice. As I said previously, I'd been really strong once – perhaps the most powerful witch the County had ever seen. But my magic had slowly faded. Giving birth to our daughter, Tilda, and fighting against powerful creatures from the dark – all that had taken its toll. Advancing age and sorrow had done the rest.

The stone tower was square and high, like the keep of a castle. It had belonged to a local knight until the abhuman had seized it for its own. I wondered if we would need to rap upon the oaken door to summon forth our bestial enemy.

But there was no need. The big door was pushed open with great force so that it banged against the wall. Then the abhuman stepped forward to confront us.

At the sight of it my heart quailed.

It was bigger than any abhuman that I'd ever seen before. And, trust me, some of them are huge with barrel chests and bursting with bulgy muscles. But this creature was twice the height of an average man. It was dressed in the skins of animals and its legs were bare, the deadly talons sprouting from the fingers and toes plain to see. As usual it was ugly with too many teeth to fit into its mouth – but there was something even worse.

Even from this distance I could feel the magic radiating from it.

It was bad.

Most abhumans had a little magic, which was usually nothing to worry about, but this one's magic was stronger than mine.

Of course, strength doesn't always guarantee victory. There are ways to exploit the slightest weakness in a stronger opponent.

I was a woman, so I knew all about that.

But first I had to find its weakness.

I walked forward. The grass surrounding the tower was littered with bones – most of them small, the remains of children that the abhuman had killed and eaten. The beast watched my approach without moving. By now it knew what I was. It would sense my magic. Getting really close to it was dangerous but necessary. The closer I got the better effect my spells would have, but the more vulnerable I would be to any counter-attack.

When we were almost near enough to touch and I could smell the stink of its unwashed hairy body and the rotting meat stuck between its teeth, I cast a spell. The creature was staring down at me without moving. My spell was working well. I had the initiative and was holding it firmly. It wouldn't do anything until I attacked.

I might just get in the first blow. So it had to be good.

If you ever fight an abhuman there's one important thing you should know. They don't like you spitting into their eyes. No one does, I suppose, but abhumans particularly hate it. The right eye is the best one to aim for. They'll lose control of any magic they hold for at least a few seconds.

It was a difficult target because the abhuman was a lot bigger and taller than me. But I'm good at spitting. Practised a lot, I have. As a girl, I was the best spitter in Pendle.

Now I spat a gob-full straight into its right eye.

It screamed with rage but I hadn't finished with it yet. Another thing about abhumans is that their ears are very sensitive. I don't mean that they can hear the faintest sounds. I mean that the *flesh* of their ears and the surrounding tissue are sensitive to pain. So it's good to hurt their ears if you can. That's good advice. Remember it!

I did just that. Easier than a pea slipping from a pod, the blade I'd hidden up my sleeve slid down into my right hand.

Then I attacked, jumping up really high towards the ugly stinky creature.

I'm old but I can still jump at least half my own height. As well as being good at spitting, I was once the best jumper in Pendle. Ain't one to brag, am I? But it was true.

I jumped high and brought the blade of my dagger down fast and hard.

I chopped off the abhuman's left ear.

Didn't like that, did it? Before its ear plopped down onto the grass it was on me, seizing me by the left shoulder. That was another mistake it made. Never grip the left shoulder of a witch! Her body reacts violently. It took me a long time to get that into Tom's head. Eventually he learned and is a lot wiser now.

My left shoulder shot about half of my remaining magic straight into the body of the beast. I hoped that would be enough to finish it.

But I was wrong.

I don't like to dwell on what happened next. But it wasn't good. I'd little left to defend myself with and it picked me up by my left leg and swung me hard against a tree. That should have smashed my skull and spread my brains all over the trunk. But I'd just enough magic left to cushion the worst of the blow and struggle to my feet.

Then the abhuman hit me hard with the back of its big left hand. It was a terrible thump that sent me spinning to my knees. I could taste blood in my mouth and this time I couldn't get up. The creature was moving towards me, holding out both taloned hands to seize my body.

I caught a whiff of its thoughts, the stink of what it intended.

It was going to tear me limb from limb.

But then there was a loud shout that caught its attention. It looked away from me towards the source of that cry.

Tom was standing lower down the slope of the hill, holding his staff at forty-five degrees, in the defensive position. He was readying himself for when the abhuman charged towards him.

'You've done enough. It's my turn now,' Tom shouted over to me.

My heart lurched with fear for Tom, but I knew that he was right. My magical strength was almost spent. Once I would have blasted this abhuman from the hill, easy-peasy. Now I needed to conserve the last bit of my power for a final defence in case we needed to escape and live to fight another day. And that day would be some time coming. It would be weeks before I was able to fight properly again.

Reluctantly, I crawled away as Tom Ward took up a position to face the abhuman. It was glaring down at the Spook and I knew that it would not use its dark magic. It would prefer to employ brute force against Tom and try to tear him apart with its bare hands. Although it usually liked young sweet flesh, it would rip some of the meat from Tom's bones to seal its victory. It was what abhumans did.

With a bestial roar it ran down the hill towards Tom, who lifted his rowan staff very slowly – so slowly that I feared he wouldn't be in time.

Had he the strength enough to grip it firmly and target the abhuman?

Then I heard the click as he released the silver-alloy retractable blade and the staff continued to rise.

Faster! Faster! I thought. To kill an abhuman you have to pierce the very centre of its forehead and drive the blade deep into its brain.

I remembered the first time I'd seen that done. Tom and I had been the prisoner of an abhuman called Tusk, and Tom's master, Old Gregory, had come to rescue us. He'd been about the same age as Tom was now but Gregory had been very fit and strong – not suffering the debilitating effects of a lung infection that had almost killed poor Tom. The abhuman had charged towards him just as this creature was doing now and the old spook had stabbed it in its forehead. It had been skilfully done and the creature had been stone dead before its big body had thumped the ground.

My heart was in my mouth as the abhuman collided with Tom. It all happened so fast that I didn't see whether or not the point of the blade made contact with the target – the only point on the creature's body that would guarantee its immediate death.

But the charge and weight of the abhuman knocked Tom clean off his feet and they fell together, the beast on top of him.

Crying out with fear for him, my heart pounding, I dashed forward, desperate to intervene and save Tom.

But I needn't have bothered myself. The abhuman was dead. The blade of the staff was buried right up to the hilt in its forehead and had pierced its brain. Tom was lying underneath it, moaning softly, his eyes closed. I seized his wrists and started to drag him clear. That done, I knelt beside him and began to stroke his face and whisper in his left ear.

After a moment or so, to my relief, he opened his eyes and smiled up at me before he began to cough. His struggle for breath went on for some time and I began to fear that he would choke, but at last the spasm ceased and he took a deep breath.

'I haven't lost my touch, have I?' he said, sitting up with a grin splitting his face. 'Thanks for softening it up.'

Walking back along the summit of the Long Ridge, within distant sight of Chipenden across the river valley, I felt a lot more cheerful. Despite it being autumn, the birds were singing, the sun was shining and we were almost home. And we'd achieved *exactly* what we set out to do. A dangerous entity from the dark was no more and we'd both avoided serious injury, living to fight another day.

'I feel a lot better, Alice, thanks to you!' Tom told me. 'A few more days and I'll be back to my old self.'

He certainly looked a lot better and now he was striding out energetically, clearly enjoying the walk. For the first time I dared to hope that he really would make a full recovery.

I knew he would be looking forward to returning to Chipenden, but not to one problem that we had left behind to be confronted with upon our return.

Tom would *not* be looking forward to being bothered by the girl again. I just called her 'the girl' because, so far, she hadn't given us her name. She'd be there now, camped by the withy trees crossroads awaiting our return. She was dark-haired, brown-eyed and very sulky. But she had determination. I'll give her that. She showed no signs at all of giving up.

Each time she approached him, Tom just waved her away, averted his eyes and refused to speak to her. She wanted to become Tom's apprentice, but that wasn't going to happen.

After all, she was female and a spook's apprentice had to be a seventh son of a seventh son. But then it became more complicated. Tom had only ever taken on one apprentice during his long career as a spook. Her name was Jenny Calder, a girl who'd claimed to be the seventh daughter of a seventh daughter. Tom had trained her for a while but sadly she'd died after being attacked by a water witch and suffering a deadly infection from a poisoned wound.

Her death had hit him hard and, after that, Tom had never taken on another apprentice. He had refused all applicants and there had been more than a few. It was something that Old Gregory his former master, who'd trained over thirty lads in his time, would have strongly disapproved of.

A spook had to train someone to replace him. That was a vital duty. The only spook still carrying out his trade in the County nowadays was Tom. All the rest were dead or gone away. Spook Johnson had gone north hunting witches but we'd had no news of him for many years. Most likely he was dead by now too – but then again he was a wily old dog, so you never knew.

If Tom didn't change his mind, something would happen. Something as plain as the nose on your face.

Tom Ward would be the last spook.

4

SOMETHING DISTURBING

Carrying a large sack of provisions over my shoulder, I climbed the hill up from the village. When I reached the withy trees crossroads it was about noon and the girl was still sitting there, almost directly under the bell used to summon the Spook.

I smiled at her and she smiled back. Then I shivered despite the warmth of the sun on my back. In that smile I suddenly saw something disturbing. That cheeky grin reminded me of Jenny, Tom's apprentice, who had been dead now for close on forty years.

It suddenly struck me there was maybe one more reason why he wouldn't take the girl on.

Had Tom noticed that likeness too?

I was tempted to go and have a word with her but thought better of it. Tom had asked me not to give her any encouragement. The sooner she gave up and went home, the easier it would be for everyone. Couldn't argue with that, could I? But I did feel a bit sorry for her.

I walked through the gap in the hedge and entered the garden. There was a faint growl in the distance from Kratch, the cat-boggart who guarded the garden and house. But it was a growl of greeting, not a warning. The boggart and I got on very well together.

I went directly to the house and left the sack on the kitchen table. Then I walked out into the garden looking for Tom. As I strolled through the trees, I could smell grass and then saw the scythe leaning against the bench that faced the fells. Tom had cut the grass – the first time since summer. That was a good sign that he was regaining his strength and energy.

There were three sections to the large garden: this pleasant area where a spook traditionally taught his apprentices on the rare days in the County when it wasn't raining, the section where rogue boggarts were bound under big heavy stones, and the area where the captured witches were imprisoned in pits.

But I could hear a faint sound in the distance that guided me to where I wanted to be. A witch like me can usually sniff out the whereabouts of somebody that they're searching for. But it didn't work on a spook because they are seventh sons of seventh sons and have some immunity against witches and dark magic.

I stayed back among the trees for a while so that I could watch Tom without disturbing him. He was practising using his silver chain, casting it again and again against the target post. Spooks had to maintain their skills by constant practice, something that had recently been denied Tom because of his illness.

But I counted each attempt. He cast it ten times, each time the silver chain finding its target. It hadn't taken him long to get back to normal.

As he collected his chain after the tenth success, I walked out of the trees towards him. He turned and smiled then stepped forward and we hugged. It felt good to be in his arms. Old as we were that didn't lessen our love for each other one jot. We were closer now than we'd ever been.

'How are you feeling?' I asked Tom. 'Ain't lost your aim, have you?'

'Didn't take long to get my eye in,' Tom said, holding me at arm's length and grinning. 'My breathing's a lot better too. Another week or so and I'll be back to my old self. The trouble is, living in the County, the cold and damp get into your bones. As you get older their effects become more severe. But I'm over it at last. Don't worry, Alice. Thanks to you I'm feeling fine and I've a good many years left to me yet.'

It was then that we heard the bell. Someone was down at the withy trees summoning the Spook.

I snatched up his bag. 'I'll take this back to the house for you while you go down and find out what the job is,' I told him. He nodded, dropped the silver chain into it, picked up his staff and set off for the crossroads.

We both knew why I'd taken his bag. That meant he'd have to come back for it before setting off on spook's business. Otherwise, if he considered it urgent, he might just leave. I wanted to make him a few butties and see if he'd mind if I went with him. When on spook's business, he usually managed with just a few mouthfuls of crumbly cheese, but after his illness he needed something more substantial to eat than that.

By the time I'd cut the bread and filled the slices with cheese and small slices of tomato and ham, Tom was back.

'Anything serious?' I asked. 'Would you like me to come with you?'

Tom shook his head. 'You're always welcome to help when there's something dangerous to deal with but there's probably nothing to this at all. Something rapping on the back door of the farmhouse at midnight – Fletcher's Farm on the lower slopes of the Long Ridge. So I should be back well before dark. I'll be fine – don't worry.'

I waved him off, gave him ten minutes and then I followed. I didn't want to seem like an old fusspot but I wasn't taking any chances. After all, Halloween was less than a week away and that witches' feast always increased dangers from the dark.

As I passed the bell at the withy trees, I noticed that the girl wasn't there. Had she gone home at last? More likely she'd followed Tom.

I remembered what Tom had once told me about Jenny. She'd done exactly the same as this girl – pestered him and followed him everywhere. He hadn't relented until she'd proved her worth by showing him the secret lair of the dangerous creature that he'd been hunting.

I set off heading south, keeping up a brisk pace. Soon I was down in the long wide Ribble Valley with Chipenden and the fells behind me and ahead, in the distance, I could see the green slopes of the Long Ridge.

Always have been a fast walker and age ain't slowed me much. I could have caught Tom easy-peasy but I was content to keep my distance. He would never know I'd followed him. For the best, that was. Tom has his pride and I didn't want to hurt him.

But I sensed that somewhere ahead was the girl and I'd decided that it was time to have it out with her. There were questions needed answering. If I was satisfied, I'd leave her be to pester Tom. There was little chance that he'd change his mind, but the girl had a right to try.

I caught up with her when we were still about a mile from Fletcher's Farm. She'd hidden herself in a small wood. No doubt she intended to waylay Tom as he returned. She had her back to me and I crept up on her slowly, making less noise than a crafty cat stalking a bird.

I'd used a small spell to make sure of that. But I was taken by surprise. I was just three paces from her when she suddenly spun round to face me, her eyes wide.

I smiled at her. 'Me and you need to talk, girl,' I told her. 'You can start by telling me your name.'

She was a pretty girl even when she frowned and now she was scowling at me, her expression darker than a County storm blustering in from Morecambe Bay.

'I don't like being sneaked up on,' she said, her eyes flashing fire.

'Don't you now?' I said, giving her a look that should have had her shaking in her shoes.

But it didn't scare her at all. She returned my gaze without flinching. Then she gave a shrug and started to walk away through the carpet of dead leaves.

I had nothing against the girl. But nobody walks away from me like that. So I cast a spell at her. A much stronger one than I'd used to take her unawares. It was like a net falling over her shoulders to pin her arms to her side and stop her from moving. Bit like the silver chain that Tom used to bind witches and just as effective. Only difference was that the net cast by my spell was invisible.

I saw her body stiffen as my net tightened but she made no sound. I walked round to face her and she glared back defiantly.

'Asked you politely, I did, and now I'm asking again, girl. Tell me your name!'

'Free me!' she said angrily.

I shook my head. 'You'll be free just as soon as you answer my questions.'

'You're making a mistake, Alice Deane,' the girl said. 'Leave me alone.'

She'd surprised me – twice.

The first surprise was in being addressed by my name like that. No doubt she could have got it from anyone down in the village. It was common knowledge that I was Alice Deane, a witch living with the Spook, Tom Ward. But she spoke my name as if she already really knew me.

The second surprise was when she broke free of my spell. She just shrugged and it shattered into thousands of pieces. But she didn't walk away. She smiled at me.

'I'll tell you my name, but I don't think you'll believe me.'

'Try me,' I said.

'My name is Jenny Calder.'

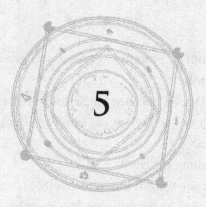

5

THE TESTING

'Tom ain't going to be happy to hear that you've called yourself that,' I said, trying not to show my own anger and dismay. 'No doubt you know about his apprentice – the poor girl who died long ago. Why have you taken her name? That's the very *last* thing that'll get you working with him. Her dying like that upset him a lot and he's never got over it. Never trained another apprentice, did he?'

'That is *my* name – not one that I've adopted. My name is Jenny Calder.'

I shook my head, still annoyed. 'If so, that's a very big coincidence, ain't it?'

She shrugged. 'It's no coincidence. I am the Jenny Calder who died after being attacked by a water witch. I've come back – I've returned to carry on from where I left off. I want to become Tom's apprentice again. I still want to train to become a spook.'

I almost slapped her face for her but then my blood ran cold. A witch can tell when somebody is lying. Not easily fooled, we are.

She was telling the truth.

Or at least she *thought* it was the truth.

And her eyes . . . the left blue, the right brown. Another coincidence? The Jenny that I remembered had possessed similarly distinctive contrasting eyes.

So I took a deep breath and calmed down. 'The Jenny Calder who was Tom's apprentice died nearly forty years ago,' I told her. 'But you're just a slip of a girl. How do you account for that?'

'I died and then I was born again just fifteen years ago. We always come back . . .'

'Who always comes back?'

'People like me.'

'What people?'

'The *Samhadre* – the *Old Ones*. We walked the earth long before you humans could even think.'

I shrugged and gave her another smile. I'd heard of the Samhadre. Some called them the *Faery*. But I'd always thought it was just a myth, a foolish story passed down through the generations. It was certainly something that spooks didn't believe in. There was nothing in Tom's library about that. But the girl wasn't lying. She really believed what she was saying.

'Let's try you with a few questions,' I told her. 'Let's see if you really are who you claim to be. Where did the first Jenny Calder live?'

'In a labourer's cottage just north of Grimsargh.'

'Lived with your parents, did you?' I asked, hoping to catch her out.

'I lived with my *foster* parents. My mother abandoned me as a baby. Left me in a nettle patch near their house and they took me in.'

'That was cruel,' I said.

'She was being cruel to be kind. My mother didn't want to be seen and was afraid to get too close to the cottage. When I got stung I cried and that was what told them there was a child out there.'

'Then who were your real parents?' I asked. This was a good test of her claim. It was possible that she could have found out about Jenny's foster parents by asking around in Grimsargh but the secret of her true parents was something that, as far as I could be sure, Jenny had only told to Tom. And, of course, later he'd told me.

'I only met my real mother just before she died. Knowing that she was dying, she came to find me and tell me what I was. She told me a little about the Samhadre too. She was one of them and their blood ran in her veins, so her gifts were passed down to me. I was going to go back and find out more but she was really sick and died before I could talk to her again.'

I nodded. This was all information almost impossible for an imposter to discover, and I could tell she wasn't lying. But I still wasn't happy so I asked something else that only the real Jenny and Tom would know.

'A Chipenden spook tests each apprentice by taking them to a haunted house in Horshaw and telling them to go down to the cellar at midnight and face the ghasts that are there. What was that test like for you?'

'I failed it. I ran.'

'So why did Tom still take you on as his apprentice?'

'After a while he came looking for me, mainly to get his tinderbox back because I had it with me when I ran. It was of sentimental value because it was a present from his dad who'd died soon after making that gift. Then he asked me why I'd run, because up until then he'd thought I was brave and unlikely to run when faced with a ghast in the cellar. So I told him. It was because of what I'd sensed about the miner and his poor wife. He was a jealous man and killed her because he thought she'd been unfaithful. But he was wrong, and as he dug the hole in the cellar to bury her, he regretted what he'd done. He still loved her and she loved him. She lay there paralysed and couldn't speak to tell him that she wasn't dead. She was terrified but loved him too. They were both full of anguish and hopelessness but they loved each other beyond measure, even as he buried her alive and she suffocated . . .'

The girl choked back a sob and I could see the tears brimming in her eyes. 'I didn't run because I was afraid,' she continued. 'One of my gifts is empathy. I knew exactly what it was like for both of them and I couldn't bear to be near such pain and tragedy. So I ran.'

I nodded. 'He gave you another chance – another test. What was it?'

'He took me into a wood where there were the ghasts of soldiers who'd been hanged during a war. I faced them, passed the test and so became his apprentice.'

'Well, girl, that's enough questions for now. Come back to Chipenden with me now and we'll talk some more. We need to do that before Tom gets back. Will you do that?'

The girl smiled. 'It would be good to see the inside of that house again. It has lots of happy memories for me.'

We turned on our heels and left the wood before continuing north towards the ford over the river. We didn't speak as we walked. I was lost in my own thoughts and that was more important than casual chit-chat.

The girl was telling the truth – I was sure of that. But it might just be what she *believed* to be the truth and that worried me.

It was possible she was a tulpa, a creature created by an enemy, crafted to do us harm.

Let me explain.

I hadn't seen my daughter, Tilda, for nearly thirty years. I blamed the company she had kept for that – a boy named Wulf. But he wasn't really human any longer. Wulf had been slain by a servant of the dark but had the power to transfer his soul into tulpas that he had created. One of them looked exactly as he had done previously but had aged at the same rate as Tilda.

When I had last seen them all those years ago, they had both been about sixteen. He and Tilda had been together since they were hardly more than children and had many adventures together. But as time went on, the protective mother instinct grew strong inside me – too strong to contain.

So I'd interfered. Said things that I shouldn't have. Minor tiffs became serious quarrels. It was mostly my fault. I admit it. Finally, I'd driven them both away. I'd heard nothing from them since. They'd probably travelled overseas, and that hurt me badly. It's one of the reasons why my hair turned white. It was all so long ago but my pain at that separation had never left me.

Wulf had his own kind of magic that was different from anything used by witches in the County. As I have explained, he could create things called tulpas.

A tulpa is a thought-form made flesh. One special type of tulpa called a 'gristle' could walk and talk, and if it had been given a human shape it believed that it really was a human being. Anyone who talked to it would believe they were human because they had been given sufficient knowledge to seem credible.

So there was a possibility that this girl, who believed that she was Jenny Calder, was actually a tulpa. Maybe she'd been sent by Wulf, or maybe someone else with similar powers. There was one way to be sure. Tom had used it many years ago against a tulpa that thought it was Bill Arkwright, a spook who used to work from the mill near the canal north of Caster.

He'd simply said to it, 'You are a tulpa!'

That had been enough to destroy it. Once a tulpa realizes that it is one, it can't bear to continue to live. It had died and fallen apart as he'd watched. So that was what I planned for the thing that thought it was Jenny. But I'd see what Tom thought first.

Once back at the house, I made both me and the girl cheese and pickle sandwiches and a hot drink of herb tea. We sat at the kitchen table while we ate. I'd noticed that there'd been no challenge from the boggart as we entered and crossed the garden. That told me that Kratch thought it was Jenny too – he only harassed strangers.

Could a boggart be fooled as easily as a human? It seemed so, didn't it?

'Do you think he'll take me on again?' the girl asked.

'That's up to Tom. But I think it best you keep out of the way while I talk to him. Why don't you go up to your old room? I'll call you down when me and Tom have had a few words.'

'It'll be good to be in that bedroom again,' she said. 'Is my name still on the wall where I added it to the rest?'

There'd been a fire many years ago and the house had burned down. It had been rebuilt but that old wall had survived. On it, every apprentice who'd ever worked for John Gregory had scrawled their name, and as Tom's first apprentice Jenny had added hers to the list.

'The room's exactly as it was,' I told her.

I watched her leave the kitchen and heard her climbing the stairs. I noticed she didn't need to be shown the way.

It was about an hour later when I heard the door open and Tom walk inside. I knew every sound he would make: leaning his staff against the wall, placing his bag next to it and the small sigh he always gave as he headed towards the kitchen, as if he was weary and glad to be back home. He wasn't breathing too hard despite the walk to the edge of the Long Ridge and back. His lungs were continuing to improve.

'How was it?' I asked as he sat opposite me at the table. I could already tell by his face that the job had not gone well.

'I wasn't able to deal with it. I'll have to go back. Maybe it's something new,' Tom said. 'The farmer said the banging at the back door occurred every Sunday at exactly the same time – midnight. There was also something else that he hadn't mentioned when we'd first spoken. Maybe he was too scared to even say it aloud. He'd described a rapping, but it was much worse than that. There were deep gouges in the wood of the door – like something had raked it with its claws. But there was more than that – the gouge marks were also scorched, as if the claws making those marks had burned it.'

Today was Monday, so we had a while until the thing returned. 'So we'll be going there next week to keep watch?' I asked.

'Yes, and I do need you with me, Alice. You might sense something that I can't. Two of us working together will be better placed to solve that problem.'

I nodded. 'We've another problem to deal with before that. The girl who wants to be your apprentice? Well, we've just had a long talk and she claims to be Jenny Calder.'

Tom's face went white with anger just as I expected. But before he could say anything, I told him the rest – what she claimed to be.

'She ain't lying, Tom. She believes every word she says. I thought that maybe she could be a tulpa. What do you think?'

'That would explain it. But why would a tulpa come here? Who would create it? Who would send it and for what purpose?'

'Wulf?' I suggested, but not really believing he would do such a thing.

Tom shook his head. 'I don't think so, Alice. I know that in the end you two didn't get along, but he was basically a good person. He wouldn't send a tulpa here in the shape of Jenny to torment me.'

'Who else would do that?' I asked.

'Who knows? We've both made enemies. It's because of who we are. Some people just don't like spooks and most folk certainly fear and hate witches. Then us being together, a witch and a spook, is enough to disturb lots of people and make them very angry. All it needs is someone with the power to make a tulpa and there are probably some with that power out there. Until Wulf met Hrothgar, the giant tulpar under the control of Circe, we'd no idea that he existed. There could be others hidden in the County who consider us to be their enemies.'

Hrothgar had trained Wulf. He'd been well hidden inside an 'underworld' that he'd created. He was very powerful, ancient and experienced. Even at the height of my powers I couldn't have entered there without being invited.

'There's one way to find out, Tom. We need to call her out.'

'It's not a nice thing to do,' said Tom. 'If that girl really is a tulpa she'll be shocked and hurt when we put her to the test. It isn't an easy death . . .'

'It still has to be done,' I said.

'If she's a gristle, the magic will have used dust, soggy leaves, twigs and maybe blood. She'll disintegrate into what she was made from. Best we do it outside in the garden,' said Tom, shaking his head sadly. I could tell that he was far from happy at the prospect of calling her out.

Some tulpas, called wraiths, were created using magic and imagination. But those that were called gristles were made from exactly what Tom said. But the ingredients could vary – some even contained ground bone and blood. Tom's actual words sounded harsh, as if he were more concerned about avoiding having the messy remains of the tulpa inside the house. But he was right and was just being practical. I knew he was sad and uncomfortable to be doing this. And it was distressing to watch.

'Call her down,' Tom said. 'Then we'll take her for a walk.'

When the girl came downstairs and confronted Tom, her eyes were bright and shining, filled with hope.

'Will you take me on as your apprentice again?' she asked.

'We need to talk first,' Tom replied. 'Let's take a walk in the garden . . .' With that he walked to the door, picking up his staff as he went. That was wise. If the tulpa had been sent to harm us it might attack at any time.

Tom led the way towards the bench and I was just a few steps behind, preparing myself for what I was about to see.

I was also gathering my magic to defend Tom and me from any threat. It looked just like a girl, but if it truly was a tulpa it might have been given dangerous powers including great strength that, under the control of the one who'd created it, the creature might use at any time.

The mild autumn weather had continued and it was a nice evening although becoming chilly now that the sun was very close to the horizon. The view of the fells was spectacular, small cloud shadows chasing each other across the fresh green slopes.

'Sit down,' Tom said to the girl.

She sat down and then smiled up at him.

Tom didn't return her smile. 'You're *not* the Jenny that I knew,' Tom said, his voice suddenly harsh.

The smile slipped from the girl's face.

'You're a tulpa!' Tom exclaimed.

The girl's whole body seemed to convulse and then she buried her face in her hands and made a strange sound. Her shoulders were shaking and shuddering. I wanted to look away but forced myself to keep my eyes upon her, dreading the change and disintegration that was about to happen.

6

THE WARNING BELL

It took me a few moments to realize what I was hearing. It was not pain or anguish at learning her true identity and facing oblivion. It was not the beginning of her disintegration. It was only as she took her hands away from her face that what I now suspected was confirmed.

Tears were streaming from her eyes but they were neither tears of sadness nor of pain.

The girl was laughing.

'You're so wrong!' she exclaimed, looking up at Tom. 'But I don't blame you for having such suspicions. Remember that I was with you, all those years ago, when you called out the tulpa who claimed to be Bill Arkwright. We were both shocked at that then, but you were right to do what you did. But not this time. I really am Jenny Calder. I've come back and I want to be your apprentice again.'

Tom and I looked at each other in surprise. A number of reactions flickered quickly over his face: astonishment, delight, hope and then happiness. If this really was the apprentice who he'd lost so long ago it would mean so much to him.

After that we walked back to the house and Tom asked her a few more questions. Neither of us could fault her answers. We had an early supper and Tom suggested that she go to bed.

'You're packing me off to bed so that you can talk over what I've said, aren't you?'

Tom shrugged and smiled. 'Of course, because we need to talk things over, Jenny,' he said, using her name for the first time. 'But you also need to spend a night in a warm bed and catch up on your sleep after so long living and sleeping outdoors. You're going to need to be wide awake tomorrow. Don't be late for breakfast. We'll start your training straight afterwards!'

She beamed at Tom. 'So you're taking me on?'

'Yes, you're now my apprentice,' Tom told her.

'Thank you, Tom,' she said as her eyes filled with tears of happiness. Then she went upstairs.

I was surprised that Tom had done that so quickly. I'd hoped that he'd discuss it with me first.

'We'll need to keep a careful watch on her,' I warned Tom once I'd heard the girl close her bedroom door. 'She still could be something else – a thing we've never encountered before. The dark is growing in power, ain't it? Its denizens will remember the things that we two have done to damage and thwart them in the past. High on that list we'll be, of all those that they hope to destroy.'

'We'll be careful and vigilant,' said Tom. 'But her claim to be one of the Samhadre could just be true. But there's nothing in the library about them. I checked all that out years ago.'

'Maybe there's nothing in that spooks' library but the Pendle witches have legends about the Samhadre,' I told him.

'And what do those legends say?' Tom asked.

'That they are reborn over and over again, but they say nothing good as far as witches are concerned. They hunted us down. Then we gathered the clans, fought back and put an end to most of them – at least in the County. But some could have survived.'

'So maybe she's exactly what she says,' Tom said.

'Sounds like she's got you convinced already, Tom,' I told him. 'Ain't blaming you for that but please take care. After all those years I don't want to lose you to a sly trick played on us by the dark. Don't take any chances. As Old Gregory used to say, "Be on your guard." Just don't take the slightest risk. Promise me?'

'I promise, Alice. If we're both alert to danger, any threat that we face will be halved. But I've got to take a chance on her. I've ignored my duty for far too long – without an apprentice I really could become the last spook. Jenny is a chance to put things right.'

I *was* alert to danger and the threat started to take shape just one day later, when Tom was in the garden – it was a sunny afternoon – with his apprentice, training her to use his silver chain. But that danger came from a different source than the one I'd anticipated.

I'd been in the library, where I occasionally went to browse the large stock of books and try to put them in a better order. Each year we got a few new ones, usually donations from the families of people who'd died. They were rarely anything directly useful to spooks when they practised their trade – nothing much about ghosts, witches and other entities – but some were about the County, with interesting personal accounts from its long history. I tended to read these and then add them to a couple of shelves that I'd reserved for that purpose.

As I was reading an autobiography by someone who'd lived in Silverdale fifty years earlier, I became aware that something had changed in the library. Something was missing. It was the absence of a particular sound.

The clock had stopped.

There was a large grandfather clock in the corner, which had been there for over twenty years. It had been given to Tom in payment for ending a difficult haunting, a problem that had taken him many visits to resolve. Below the clock face was a tall cabinet with a glass front. Inside it was a pendulum which was no longer swinging.

It took me just seconds to sort it out. I opened the cabinet, gave the brass pendulum a sideways nudge and the clock carried on as if nothing had happened. I watched it for a couple of minutes until I was satisfied – it seemed to be working fine.

But I wasn't happy, was I? I felt that I had been warned in some way. It felt as if something with a long invisible arm had reached into the garden, bypassing the boggart, then moved inside the house, into the library and stopped the clock.

The *tick-tock* of that clock suddenly halting made me think of a heart ceasing to beat. Tom and I had been happy. Was our time together finally coming to an end?

I shrugged it off and went out into the garden, already having decided not to mention it to Tom. Why worry him when it was little more than a gloomy feeling – nothing that I could be sure of?

Tom and the girl were down by the post where he'd be making her cast the chain at it over and over again until she started to improve. I could hear their voices in the distance.

I walked through the trees until I reached my herb garden. My plants were still growing slowly but the first serious frost would soon put an end to them. I plucked some leaves – just those that might help to strengthen Tom and lower the risk of his bad chest coming back.

It was then that I heard the bell ringing down at the withy trees. I sniffed and I didn't like what I found. Witches like me can usually sniff out a lot when I'm close to somebody. I can learn the important things about 'em. That's called *short-sniffing*. But there's another kind of sniffing that it's best not to rely upon too much.

It's called *long-sniffing* and it tells you what *might* happen in the future. But nothing is certain and it's no better than scrying with a mirror. You think you see clearly what's going to happen but then ten minutes later somebody makes a decision or does something and the future changes again. Ain't nothing fixed, is there? We make the future minute by minute so I ain't much faith in long-sniffing even though I do it anyway, mostly out of habit.

But sometimes the sniff tells you something a bit different. It's rare but it does happen. It warns you about something that won't change that much. Something that *can't* change much.

I sniffed danger. Whatever kind of danger it was, I hadn't a clue, but whatever job that bell was summoning Tom for wasn't good.

By now he'd be on his way down to the crossroads with the girl to find out what needed doing. But I made up my mind right away that, whatever it was, I'd be going with them. Even if it seemed simple and routine there was no way that I'd let Tom talk me out of it.

There was danger for sure and I wanted to be there to help. That was no ordinary ringing.

It was a warning bell.

'There are two jobs need doing,' Tom said as he walked into the kitchen with the girl. 'So we need to be up at first light tomorrow. If we're lucky we'll get there before dark. We're going southwest of Priestown close to the big sea marsh on the southern bank of the River Ribble.'

'Two jobs?' I asked. 'Were there two people down at the crossroads?'

'No, Alice, just one. They'd sent a boy. I invited him up to the house to stay overnight but I think young Danny was a bit nervous because Jenny kept winking at him.'

'No, I didn't!' the girl declared, slapping playfully at Tom's shoulder.

They seemed easy with each other. That worried me. Tom seemed to have let his guard down already.

'So, two jobs from the same location?' I asked.

'Not exactly but they aren't that far apart. Both jobs are being paid for by the landlord of the Black Bull Inn at Churchtown. One is just a straightforward haunting – a ghost that walks a lane in a village called Banks. The other might be more of a problem – it's happening at the inn itself.

And it's exactly the same as what I found at Fletcher's
Farm – hard rapping at the back door of the inn at midnight
and gouges in the woodwork.'

'Then I'll be coming with you,' I told him firmly.

Tom didn't try to protest because he knew he'd be wasting
his time. When I make up my mind to do something, nobody
gets in my way – not even Tom.

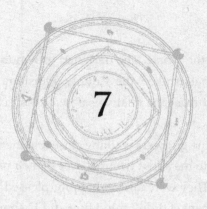

7

RALPH'S WIFE

The sun was barely clear of the horizon when we set off. But the boggart had made us a tasty breakfast and, fortified by that, we made good progress. We forded the Ribble near the village of Ribchester and continued along the river's southern bank.

As we neared Priestown, we moved further south to keep well clear of it. I could see the cathedral spire jutting up into the sky, its white limestone bricks gleaming in the sun. That town was one of the most dangerous places in the whole of the County for both a spook and a witch, but not just because of threats from the dark. Church Quisitors operated from there, and if we fell into their cruel hands we'd be tortured, have a very short trial and then be burned at the stake.

Of course, at the moment we were probably safer than we had ever been. Over the last twenty years or so things had changed for the worse. The dark had grown in power and, afraid of what walked the County, Quisitors only rarely ventured out from the relative safety of their churches and abbeys.

Tom and the girl were walking close together, shoulder to shoulder, with me about twenty paces to their rear, guarding their backs. They were talking happily, pleased to be in each other's company. I didn't mind that, did I? Tom had perked up so much once he'd accepted that it really was Jenny. Despite lots of scary encounters with the dark, losing his first and only apprentice had probably been one of the worst things that had happened to him as a spook. Now he considered her to be back, it had lifted his spirits no end.

But I was not so easily convinced. I was still on guard, ready for the slightest threat from the girl. If that threat never reared its ugly head, all well and good. But if it did, then I'd be ready.

Once well clear of Priestown we stopped to eat the cheese and ham butties that I'd packed for us. As we set off again the weather was beginning to change, the sun becoming covered with grey clouds. There was little wind and soon a mist began to form.

There was sea marsh ahead to our right and then a big lake called Martin Mere to our left, surrounded by its own reed-shrouded bog. So we needed to walk with care. But I was happy to let Tom lead the way. Spooks weren't called that much to this part of the County, but I knew that Tom had been to Ormskirk two or three times and had also visited the hamlet of Crossens, which should now be directly in our path. We were walking slower because the going was difficult. Twice we had to circle back and skirt boggy ground, and even walking the main track mostly had us ankle-deep in mud.

We reached Crossens early in the evening before the sun went down. Not much to it, just a dozen cottages and a chapel, but soon after that the mist lifted and we came in sight of Churchtown, which was slightly larger. Its church was easily the biggest building, far too large for a village that size. And there were two unusual things about it. The first was that it had a steeple. It wasn't as impressive as Priestown Cathedral – perhaps no more than a quarter of the size – but it was very slim and pointed. The second was that the church was no longer in use.

You could tell that by the way its main door had been boarded up with thick planks of wood. Most of the windows were smashed too – even two stained-glass ones that were usually very expensive.

Churchtown was right on the edge of the marsh, the sea grass covered by about a foot of tide, but there were deep channels that led out into the Ribble estuary and over a dozen or so fishing boats were moored there. We got a few curious glances as we walked into the village but none of them were particularly unfriendly. Here, everybody would know each other's business and this visit from the Spook was expected.

Finding the Black Bull proved to be easy. It was black-beamed with whitewashed walls and shone brightly, reflecting the bright light of the setting sun into our eyes. Set on the far edge of the village green, it was a large building with extensive stables to the side.

'Wouldn't think there'd be much need for a coaching house here,' I said to Tom.

'You'd be surprised,' he said. 'There's a daily coach from Liverpool to Ormskirk that calls here first. It carries passengers but also picks up fish to be delivered there fresh the same day. Then in summer two coaches a day run directly through to Priestown.'

As we approached the inn, a man came out to greet us. 'I am Henry Jackson, the innkeeper of the Black Bull!' he announced a little pompously, full of self-importance.

I suppose it was a good thing that he said who he was because I'd never have guessed that he was the innkeeper. Most that I'd seen usually wore a mucky ale-stained apron and often had bellies big enough to make a porky bishop jealous, because of all the drink they slurped while serving customers. Henry Jackson was a dapper little man who dressed like a wealthy landowner with a white shirt, a waistcoat, dark trousers and polished shoes.

'I'm Tom Ward, the Chipenden Spook, and this is my apprentice Jenny and my wife Alice.'

Tom always introduced me to strangers as his wife. Although we'd never stood before a priest and didn't need the blessing of the Church, Tom was my husband and I was his wife. It was enough that we said it was so to each other.

'No sense in wasting time,' said the innkeeper, glancing down at our muddy shoes. 'Let me show you our back door and what's been done to it.'

He led us round the outside of the building and showed us the damaged back door.

'Pretty much the same has happened to a farmhouse that I visited recently,' said Tom.

There were deep gouges in the wood clearly made by claws. There was evidence of burning too. You could see it and smell it.

'So you've seen something like this before?' Henry Jackson asked.

Tom nodded. 'Yes, at Fletcher's Farm close to the Long Ridge, not that far from where we live.'

'Did you manage to sort the problem?' asked Henry.

'Not yet. I was told that it happens once each week on the same day – Sunday. My plan was to be there on the spot when it happened again. But as I'm here I'll deal with this first.'

'Happens every week here too but on a different day. Friday.'

'Well, that's just two days away, so it's best if I deal with a different haunting first. That's in a village called Banks, I was told.'

Henry nodded. 'That haunting has been going on for years and it didn't bother folks much but now things have changed. There are two ghosts now and something even worse. But I'd best let someone who's been a witness to that tell you about it. He's a far better way with words than I have and he'll be here soon to sing for his supper. Talking of supper . . . will you be wanting to stay here at my inn?'

'I'd like to, that's if you have vacancies – two rooms, if possible.'

'That's done easy enough. Don't have many customers since that trouble at my back door. It was loud and woke up half the village. So I'll tell you what, Mr Ward. Sort out both problems for me and your accommodation and food will be on the house in addition to your fee. What do you say to that?'

'It's very generous of you, Mr Jackson,' Tom said, stepping closer and shaking his hand.

So the bargain was struck and Tom and I took one room and Jenny the other smaller one. Once Tom would have been happy to make himself comfortable sleeping outdoors and it would have been enough for me too, but those days were long gone. As Tom often said, the County was damp even at the best of times and the cold got deep into your bones.

Both rooms were comfortable and after we'd washed and chatted for a while all three of us went down the narrow stairs and entered the dining area. It wasn't much, just a few tables to the side of the bar, but it gave a good view of the empty room with its curtained windows and large candles on iron brackets affixed to the wall. There was a big fire blazing in the grate too so we were warm enough.

The food was plain but plentiful, a hotpot with a thick gravy and even thicker crust which we washed down with a small glass of ale each. As we ate, the room began to fill up with locals – all of them men – and Henry Jackson was kept busy serving jugs of ale. He was still wearing his dapper clothes, a spotless white shirt and waistcoat, which was a great contrast with his customers. Judging by the way they dressed, they were mostly fishermen dressed in the boots, mucky woollens and waterproofs of their trade.

As I was mopping up the last bit of tasty gravy, a young minstrel entered the room and took up position with his back to one of the large curtained windows.

'It's young Danny, the boy you took a liking to,' Tom teased the girl.

Before she could reply, without any introduction Danny strummed his guitar and began to sing a sea shanty.

A few people turned their backs to the bar and faced towards him. He was a good-looking boy with fair hair and a broad friendly face. He played well but his voice was very ordinary and sometimes he seemed to be talking rather than singing. When he came to the end of his third song Henry Jackson made a great show of clapping and his customers were quick to follow his lead and join in the applause.

In the moments of silence that followed, Henry turned towards us. 'Mr Ward, Danny here is the witness that I was talking about earlier and he's written a song about what he saw. Tell them what you've called it, Danny . . .'

Danny nodded towards us. 'I've called it "Ralph's Wife",' he said. Then he began to strum the introduction and the room fell silent as we listened to his song.

8

DANNY'S SONG

It was a strong ballad and the young man's voice seemed to deepen and grow richer and more tuneful as he strummed his guitar and sang.

> '*Down the lane the white ghost walks*
> *I turn not in fear and dread*
> *For though she's hunting for my soul*
> *To this place I have been led*
>
> *She's waiting for her husband, Ralph*
> *A smuggler lost at sea*
> *He's drowned and dead*
> *Most folks believe*
> *Ralph's wife does not agree*

The Last Spook

I see her pause beside the hedge
Tears falling from her eyes
Her whole soul is wracked with grief
With a love that never dies

When she sees me close to her
She sobs and cries aloud
For she can tell that I'm dead too
But I wear no burial shroud

My hair is wet, my garments drenched
Water squelches in my shoes
It tastes of salt within my mouth
And from my ears doth ooze

I was a smuggler lost at sea
But now as a ghost I walk
Her love hath brought me to this lane
But there's no time to stand and talk

Across the salt marsh, now we glide
Together hand in hand
We reach the margin of the sea
And move across the sand

But this is no happy tale
No cosy ending here
For a ship is now close to shore
Its look fills me with fear

Its crew they stare towards me
Eyeballs melting on their cheeks
The sails are torn
The rigging worn
I am the soul they seek

For I must pay for all my sins
I wish there were but few
Now bound in shackles, hand and foot
I must join that grisly crew

I'll set sail for lands unknown
My wife must stay behind
For I must suffer for each sin
My fate will not be kind!'

Everyone clapped including Tom, the girl and me, but this time the applause from the fishermen was strangely muted and Danny didn't play again. He leaned his guitar against the wall and joined the fishermen at the bar. Henry Jackson brought him a mug of ale and a plate of steaming hotpot.

'So he's just sung about what he actually saw?' asked Jenny, her eyes wide.

Tom shrugged. 'Maybe,' he said. 'Or what he *thinks* he saw. Witnesses who claim to see ghosts aren't usually that reliable. He could be exaggerating too for the purpose of creating a good ballad. Not only did he sing about two ghosts together, which is very unusual, but there was also a ship full of the dead. That all makes for a good entertaining story but it's not necessarily what we'll be dealing with. We need to talk to him.'

Tom's wish was soon granted, because no sooner had he finished his plate of hotpot than Danny walked towards the table, carrying his mug of ale.

'May I join you?' he asked politely.

Tom smiled and nodded. 'Of course,' he said, gesturing towards our table. 'This is my wife, Alice. You've already met Jenny.'

'Pleased to meet you, Danny,' I said, smiling at him.

The young man drew up a chair and sat facing Tom, but it was Jenny who spoke first.

'I enjoyed your songs, Danny,' she said. 'Especially the last one.'

'Thank you. It's nice to be appreciated. It's a pleasure to meet you all.'

'I enjoyed your song too,' said Tom, 'but I have to ask you – how much is based upon what you saw and how much did you add and exaggerate to make it a good ballad that would please and interest an audience?'

'Some of it I added to make a better ballad of it,' Danny replied, smiling. 'For example, I sing it from the perspective of Ralph the drowned ghost but I've no way of really knowing what goes on inside his head. When I saw the ghost it made no sound at all. And I've no sure way of knowing that it was him. But the two ghosts and the big boat I certainly did see.'

'Was Ralph really a smuggler?' asked Tom.

'Some say a smuggler, others say a pirate. But maybe he was just a poor fisherman drowned at sea. The place where I saw the ghosts is called "Ralph's Wife's Lane" and it got its name from the ghost of the woman who's been seen walking that lane for many a long year. Folks believe that she's waiting for the return of her husband Ralph who was lost at sea. As the story goes, she used to walk that lane while she was still alive, hoping against hope that he wasn't dead and that one day he would return to her. And now she's dead she carries on in the same way.'

'Had you seen her ghost before?' asked Tom.

'Probably half a dozen times or so. My mother still lives in a cottage down at the end of that lane and I visit her regularly. So, yes, I've glimpsed the ghost maybe six or seven times in as many years. But this was different. When I saw her before she was barely visible – just a faint luminous grey – but this time she glowed brightly. So I crossed the road to get a better look . . .'

'Weren't you scared?' asked Jenny. 'It was a brave thing to do – especially when you were alone.'

'I was full of ale,' Danny answered with a smile. 'Almost too much in my cups to remember what fear was. Besides, the ghost has never harmed anyone before. She's just sad and taken up with her own grief – that's what people believe. But no sooner had I crossed the lane to get a better look than a second ghost appeared. He was dressed like a fisherman and I could see water cascading from his body and drenching the ground. But when I looked closely, the ground was dry – or at least as dry as it gets to be this late in the autumn.'

'So you followed them?' Tom prompted.

'That I did. I was far too drunk to know what was good for me. I followed them across the lane then onto the path through the salt marsh towards the estuary. Then I saw the ship and for the first time I was scared . . .'

'Was it exactly as you described?'

'Not really,' said Danny. 'I needed to describe the ship and crew in rhyme so the line "Eyeballs melting on their cheeks" gave me the rhyme I needed for "I am the soul they seek". The crew shone just as brightly as Ralph and his wife but their eyes certainly weren't sliding down their cheeks. That was just made up. But the terrifying thing was that they weren't looking at Ralph and his wife. They were staring at *me*.'

'So you ran?' prompted Tom.

'Not right away,' Danny replied. 'I was frozen to the spot. My limbs wouldn't obey me. The crew looked a right rough bunch. They wore tattered clothes and I didn't like the expressions on their faces. That was the worst thing – the way they glared at me. They had the shapes of men but they seemed more like demons to me – things that didn't belong in this world.'

I took a subtle sniff, doing it so quietly and carefully that nobody noticed. I was long-sniffing, testing the future. Once again I sensed danger. And I knew that the threat came from that ghostly ship.

'Did Ralph board the ship the way you suggested in your song?' asked Tom.

'No,' said Danny. 'That's something else I made up. They just vanished, the ship, its crew and the two ghosts that I'd followed. Suddenly I was free to move so I ran all the way to my mother's house. And that's not all. Before that night, it was often weeks before Ralph's wife could be seen haunting the lane again. Now both ghosts walk the lane *every* night. Other folks have seen them since and people are getting scared. It needs sorting out.'

'Well, that's what we're here for,' said Tom. 'Will you guide us to the lane and the place where you saw the ghosts?'

'Tonight?' asked Danny.

'No, better make it tomorrow,' I said, speaking for the first time. Knowing Tom, he'd be keen to sort that spook's business as soon as possible. But he needed his rest. 'We've been walking all day to get here and we're tired,' I explained. 'Tomorrow, after a good night's sleep, we'll be better able to deal with the problem.'

'Tomorrow night it is,' said Danny. 'Usually, the ghosts walk the lane in the hour before midnight. So if we meet here about ten that should give us plenty of time to get there. But just one thing . . . I'm happy to show you to the place where the ghosts walk but after that you're on your own. I don't want to go anywhere near that ship again.'

Tom smiled. 'That's agreed.'

With that, Danny left us and we came to our feet ready to go up to our beds.

We paused outside Jenny's room. 'You've seen ghosts sent to the light before and you've tried it yourself,' Tom told her. 'But this time there are two, which makes things a lot more difficult – not to mention the ship and its crew. So I think I'd better deal with this. Just watch closely what I do and afterwards write it all up in your notebook. You'll get another chance to deal with a ghost soon enough.'

She grinned at him cheekily. 'Of course, master, I hear and obey!'

Jenny Calder had always been a bit cheeky and disrespectful. Old Gregory would never have allowed an apprentice to get away with that. But, of course, he wouldn't have taken on a girl in the first place. Her attitude didn't bother Tom in the slightest. He smiled and took it as a joke which, of course, it was.

'Sleep tight!' he joked back. 'Mind the boggarts don't bite!'

She grinned again and went into her room.

I'd been worried about the journey taxing Tom's strength. But he seemed fine and fell asleep the moment that his head touched the pillow. But I lay there for a long time thinking about the two ghosts and the ship. Before arriving here, I'd been more concerned about the thing from the dark that had gouged the back door of the inn and probably the door of Fletcher's Farm too. But now that faded into second place.

What worried me now was the two ghosts that haunted Ralph's Wife's Lane and, above all, that ship. I couldn't get it out of my mind.

That ship was the biggest threat I'd sniffed out in many a year.

9

THE SHIP OF DEMONS

We got up and had a lazy day with a very late breakfast and an early supper. Tom and I walked the area a bit to get our bearings while Jenny went off on her own. The tide was low at noon so we went down a mud track through the salt marsh to the bank of the river. It was a wide estuary. The water seemed distant, the mudflats gleamed in the sun and there was a strong tang of the sea.

Far across the river there were cottages, almost too small to see. I knew that was either a village called Lytham or the hamlet near the Black Pool but I wasn't sure which. They were somewhere on the north bank or beyond it, facing the Irish Sea.

When we returned to the inn, the girl was sitting outside on a bench, having an animated conversation with young Danny. It seemed that she made friends easily. But she left him as soon as we arrived and joined us for supper.

'You're not happy with me, Alice,' she said as we finished off our fish and peas supper. 'I could see you scowling at me when I was talking to Danny. I don't think you liked me being with him.'

Perhaps I had been scowling but I hadn't meant to. But the girl was certainly blunt and not afraid to speak her mind.

'Ain't no problem for me, girl, who you spend your time with,' I told her.

'I hope you mean that, Alice,' she said, a sad expression on her face. Then she lowered her voice as she continued to speak. 'It's just that my last life was really short and I didn't make the most of it. Nobody knows what lies ahead and I want to enjoy this life while I can. I like being with Danny. He makes me happy.'

'And when you go back to Chipenden and leave him? How happy will you feel then?' I asked, speaking my mind also.

'I'll go back to Chipenden when that time arrives,' she said. 'You needn't concern yourself about that.'

I nodded. There was nothing more I could say. Until I had proof otherwise, I had to accept that the girl was exactly who she claimed to be and had to exist with her on the best terms we could manage. I noticed that Tom had kept out of the conversation.

Fierce as he was when facing the dark or anyone else who threatened him directly, Tom didn't like confrontations with people – especially family. It had been a big disappointment that he hadn't sided with me more when my rows with my daughter and Wulf began. He'd just done his best to keep the peace. That was Tom and there was no changing him. It was useless to try.

We set off at ten as we'd agreed, Danny being our guide. We needed him too because there was neither moon nor stars to light our way. The cloud cover above was thick and another mist was starting to form, tendrils of it writhing at our feet.

We passed through the village of Banks without hardly noticing it. Nothing much to it, there was – just a narrow road with a dozen or so houses and a dilapidated inn in darkness. I glimpsed a crumbling wall and boarded-up doors and windows, showing that it had been abandoned. We came to another lane and turned left.

'This is the lane,' Danny whispered. 'The ghosts are usually seen a bit further along among the trees on the left . . .'

So we kept to the left side of the lane, walking into the trees following Danny, our pace gradually slowing. On the other side of the lane we saw the odd cottage but all were in darkness.

'Where's your mother's house?' Tom asked, keeping his voice low.

'Long way ahead,' said Danny. 'Right at the end of the lane. And I'll be off there as soon as we see the ghosts. Ah, look! There's the first of them,' he said, lowering his voice and pointing ahead.

I could see the luminous figure of a woman a little way ahead among the trees. She was walking directly towards us. She wore a long dress that came down to her ankles and her hair was long, draped across her shoulders. The ghost had no colour at all but was far brighter than any apparition I'd ever seen before.

'I'll be off now,' said Danny, giving us a wave. 'See you tomorrow, Jenny!' Then he crossed the lane, walking at speed towards his mother's cottage.

Tom took a few steps forward and to the side to place himself directly in the path of the ghost. I could see the woman's face now. She was pretty and appeared to be no older than thirty. But her face was twisted into a mask of grief and I could see the tears flowing from her eyes and dripping from her chin.

'We need to talk,' Tom said to the ghost, his voice gentle and calm. 'I'm here to help you and take away your sorrow. There's a better place for you than this.'

But the ghost didn't respond. It kept walking forward as if he wasn't standing in her way. She passed straight through Tom's body and continued onwards.

Tom turned and glanced towards Jenny. 'It's not a ghost,' he said. 'It's a ghast.'

There was a big difference between a ghost and a ghast. The former was a soul trapped on earth. With careful words, a spook could usually send it to the light. Tom had done that many times. The ghost usually responded to a seventh son of a seventh son and listened to what he said. After winning its confidence a spook usually asked the spirit to think about a happy time during its time on earth. That was often all that was needed to send it onwards. Tom was very good at that. He'd probably lost count of the number of ghosts that he'd sent to the light.

But ghasts were far different. In that case, the spirit of the dead person had already gone to the light. The ghast was all that remained. It was just a discarded fragment of either someone once tormented by something unbearable or else guilty of a crime. The miner in the cellar, where Tom had tested Jenny, was a ghast. So was the wife he was burying alive. And you couldn't communicate with a ghast. They just went on walking the same route in an endless pattern. They were an unaware fragment of a former ghost. They did not speak or think. They could not react to anything.

A spook could not get rid of a ghast. Henry Jackson would not be pleased about that.

'Let's wait a while and see if everything happens just as Danny described,' said Tom.

The ghast of the woman took no more than a dozen steps beyond us before it turned and headed back in our direction.

It passed us less than an arm's length away, completely unaware of our presence, and then continued into the trees, each step taking her further from us.

As Tom had said, the ghost of Ralph's wife had no awareness. It was a mindless thing haunting this lane. Just as she'd spent a long time walking here hoping for the return of her husband, now the ghost repeated that. But how had the two entities come to be together when it seemed that Ralph had actually drowned far away from this lane? That puzzled me.

There was something new and different here.

We began to follow the ghost, walking slowly behind and keeping our distance. Then, suddenly, another luminous figure appeared, this one male and dressed in the garb of a sailor. I thought they might have halted but they hardly paused and within moments, walking side by side, crossed the dark lane and started to move quickly. I wondered if the male figure was a ghost too. There'd be no way of checking that until we got closer.

We followed, but suddenly I couldn't see them any longer. I realized they'd left the lane and taken a narrow path that led towards the salt marsh.

We took that same path, Tom in the lead, the girl between us. I could hear our shoes squelching through the mud and sometimes a shoot from the hedge to my right brushed against my face or hair. But it was very dark and I could hardly see anything at all but for the glow of the two spirits ahead of us.

We must have walked for at least five minutes but then I could see that the sky ahead was lit up as if the moon was about to rise. But we were facing roughly north and I knew that it was the wrong direction for a rising moon and the clouds were too thick anyway. I began to feel dread like a heavy weight in the pit of my stomach because I already knew what must be illuminating the sky.

We were approaching the ghost ship.

Suddenly there it was, directly in front of us, far larger than I'd expected. I could see three masts and rigging and the furled sails. Moments later we reached the end of the muddy track.

There was no sign of the two glowing figures we'd followed. They'd vanished but the ghost ship was immediately ahead of us, tied up to a dilapidated wooden wharf. Its glow had diminished and now it was illuminated by a wan, sickly yellow light.

The crew were staring at us and Danny's description had been accurate. Human in shape, they looked rough and dishevelled. They wore the clothes of sailors but they were tattered and torn. However, it was their eyes that drew my own gaze. They were filled with malevolence. The crew of that ship hated us and wanted to hurt us very badly.

So what were they? Ghosts, ghasts or something else?

Danny had thought them demons. It was a word that spooks rarely used because it was imprecise, covering many different spirit entities including bugganes, harpies and Romanian demons such as the strigoi which were vampires.

All types of demon were much more powerful than boggarts and could talk and scheme, often using their wiles to ensnare humans. Some were ascending, gradually growing more powerful, hoping to become gods, while others were falling and weakening. The Bane, once trapped below Priestown Cathedral and bound behind a silver gate, had also been a type of demon. Once it had been a god and wanted to become one again. Before that happened, I had helped Tom and Old Gregory to destroy it. But that was many years ago. I needed to concern myself with the here and now.

So were these glowing human-shaped figures some type of dangerous demon?

There were a couple of dozen of them and if they truly were demons they were the biggest threat that had visited our world in many years.

It was then that my eye was drawn to one of them, which was much larger than the others. It wore a black cloak that was fastened at the neck and a hood that was pulled low on the forehead, obscuring its face but for the eyes that burned like orbs of fire. Standing next to that hooded creature was another tall demon which had three eyes, the largest one right in the middle of its forehead. Then, as I watched, the hooded demon reached up with its left hand and pulled the hood back and down onto its shoulders to reveal its whole head. I was so shocked that I staggered back and almost fell. I recognized that broad malevolent face. I stared in horror at the curved ram's horns jutting from the large head.

It was the Fiend.

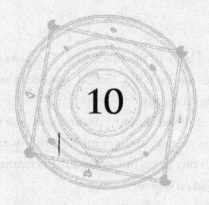

10

ALL COME TO NOTHING

There was a rumble of thunder directly overhead and very suddenly the ship vanished.

We didn't move but just stared in silence at the place where it had been. The water was flat and calm, completely undisturbed. There was no evidence at all that something so big had been there, nor any sign of the rope that had tethered it to a post. The boat had been insubstantial, like the ghost that had walked through Tom. Now it had gone.

But the entities standing on the deck had not been ghosts – of that much I was certain.

Tom was the first to speak. 'Let's get back to the inn,' he said. 'This is no place to linger and we need to decide what to do next.'

We trudged back to the Black Bull, Tom leading the way. But once we reached the lane, I walked alongside him holding his hand tightly.

I was afraid. I had thought dealing with the abhuman at Salford had been very dangerous and full of risk. We had gambled with our lives. But everything screamed out at me that this was even worse.

Back at the inn we tried to be as quiet as possible as we climbed the stairs. Tom signalled to his apprentice that she should follow us into our room. Once there, Tom and I sat next to each other on the bed while Jenny took our only chair.

'The spirit of the woman in the lane was certainly a ghost,' said Tom, 'but I'm not sure about her companion or the crew aboard that ship. They stared at us. They seemed aware of us. Danny called them demons and I don't think he's that far off the mark. Ghosts don't usually congregate like that.'

I was surprised that Tom hadn't mentioned the Fiend.

'Most likely they were some type of demon,' I said. 'Ain't much doubt about that. Fitting company they were for the Fiend.'

'You saw the Fiend?' Tom asked, his eyes widening in astonishment.

'Didn't *you*?' I asked.

Tom shook his head. Jenny's gaze flicked from me to Tom and back to me again. Her eyes showed nervousness and a hint of fear.

'He was there among the crew,' I said. 'He was bigger than any of them and wore a hood to hide his face. But his eyes were glowing red. Then he pulled the hood right back. That big skull, the curved ram's horns – I'd know them anywhere. It was the Fiend all right. He's back – ain't no denying it.'

The Fiend had once been the most powerful of the Old Gods and also the ruler of the dark. Tom had destroyed him many years ago, but if enough humans still believed, it was possible for such an entity to return.

'Did you see him, Jenny?' Tom asked.

'I was terrified,' the girl said. 'I only saw that terrible crew with their staring eyes – in particular one of them with three eyes, the third one huge and right in the centre of its forehead. But I didn't see what Alice described.'

'Maybe he only showed himself to you, Alice,' Tom said. 'So why would he do that?'

I shrugged. 'I ain't got any idea,' I said. 'But one thing I am certain of. We should get ourselves back to Chipenden while we still can.'

Tom frowned. 'You know I can't do that, Alice. I've never walked away from spook's business before.'

'This is different, Tom. Ain't you able to see that? First of all, you can do nothing about the ghast woman, and her companion is probably a ghast too. And how are you going to deal with that ghost ship? Not true ghosts, are they? So you can't persuade 'em to go to the light. They're some type of demon, for want of a better word, and may not even be solid so your staff ain't going to be much good. Then if the Fiend really is back . . .'

I left the consequences unsaid. Tom had played a big part in destroying the Fiend. Had Tom failed, the Fiend would have walked the earth in the flesh and a new age of darkness would have begun. Now that threat loomed over us again.

'Did you sense anything from them, Jenny? Any hint at what was in their minds?' Tom asked.

The Jenny who'd been Tom's apprentice forty years earlier had a gift of empathy – as she had shown on her first test. Something special. Could this girl do the same?

She shook her head. 'From the two who walked the lane, I got nothing. But I could sense malevolence and hatred from those monsters on the ship. And I got no hint at all of what they really were.'

'Things might seem clearer in the morning,' Tom said. 'We should get a good night's sleep. But I know one thing for sure: we need to be here tomorrow night to deal with whatever banged on the back door of the inn and gouged it with its claws. Well, Jenny,' he said, coming to his feet and smiling at her, 'get yourself off to bed. We'll discuss this again tomorrow.'

Jenny didn't argue. She wished us both goodnight and then went to her own room.

Tom closed the door behind her; then he gave a long weary sigh.

'A penny for them,' I said.

'It's just . . . Well, Alice, if the Fiend really is back, then it makes me feel that my whole life as a spook has been a failure. It's all come to nothing.'

I was surprised to hear him talk so. 'You're tired, Tom, and ain't thinking clearly. You've achieved a lot – probably at least as much as Old Gregory and that's saying something. Not only has the County been free of the Fiend for forty years or more but you've damaged or slain so many other entities from the dark too. You've hurt the dark badly and that's no small thing!'

He gave a grim smile. 'That's true enough, Alice. But it feels like I deal with one threat from the dark and another grows in strength to take its place. And this is worse. The most powerful-ever creature from the dark looks to be back. If that's the case, when I die things will be worse than when I first became John Gregory's apprentice.'

I tried to cheer him up but got nowhere. Despite his gloomy thoughts and worries, Tom dropped off to sleep quickly. He was still feeling the debilitating after-effects of his illness. His body needed all the sleep that it could get.

I was the one who lay awake half the night, my head whirling with what we faced.

Nobody spoke much at breakfast but Jenny certainly hadn't lost her appetite. She wolfed down her eggs and bacon as if she hadn't eaten for a month.

It was as we were about to stand and go back to our rooms that Henry Jackson came across. Without a word he grabbed a chair and rudely invited himself to join our company.

'How did it go last night, Mr Ward? Did you deal with the first of our two little problems?' he asked.

'I'm sorry to say it isn't a little problem,' Tom said. 'I can do nothing about at least one of the two spirits that haunt the lane in Banks because it's what we call a ghast. They are harmless but persistent and there is nothing that a spook can do about them. What worries me more is the ghost ship. I've never dealt with anything like that before – so many entities from the dark gathered in one place. That certainly does need sorting out but at the moment I'm not quite sure how to proceed.'

Jackson frowned. 'That's very disappointing, Mr Ward. I expected far more from a spook with your experience and reputation. But at least you're honest and haven't tried to make excuses. What about my own problem here? After that setback, will you at least try to deal with that?'

'Yes, I'll do my best. Tonight we'll confront whatever gouged that door.'

'Well, let's hope you have more success than with the other matter,' said Jackson, an edge of sarcasm in his voice. Then, without another word, he left us and strode away towards the kitchen.

'That was uncalled for – and really rude!' Jenny said. 'People don't have a clue how difficult and dangerous a spook's job is.'

'He's probably just worried about his business,' Tom said. 'But you're right, Jenny. Most folk have no idea about what we face and how great the danger sometimes is – not just to us but also to each community nearby. And maybe that's a good thing or they wouldn't sleep easily in their beds at night.'

I knew Tom was just being nice. He saw no point in picking an argument with Henry although I'd been close to giving him a piece of my mind.

'Well,' Tom said, 'as we've plenty of time before tonight, I'd like to take another look at that wharf where we saw the ship – this time in daylight.'

Despite the mist of the previous evening and night, the weather had been dry for well over a week. But now it had gone back to typical County weather and we walked towards Banks, gradually getting soaked by a heavy drizzle.

When we arrived at the wharf, I couldn't rid myself of the memory of the ghost ship that we'd seen the night before. It was the glaring eyes of the crew that had burned themselves into my head. I don't scare easily but I was glad it was daylight with little chance of those things from the dark visiting this place again.

The estuary was calm but the rain was still drifting across the water and, as I glanced back towards the land, I saw something that I hadn't noticed the night before. It had been hidden by trees and cloaked in darkness.

But I saw it clearly now. Just beyond the edge of the wharf there was a large wooden building leaning away from the water as if it were about to fall over. It must have once been a busy warehouse where goods were stored ready to be loaded onto ships. Now, judging by the dilapidated state of the wharf, with its missing timbers and the ones remaining mostly rotten, it was clear enough that trade and prosperity had left Banks far behind.

Without anybody saying a word we walked towards the warehouse, trudging through soggy brown leaves. No doubt we all had the same idea. It would at least provide some shelter from the rain.

Once inside there was the smell of damp wood and rot. It was gloomy, and it took a while for my eyes to adjust. It was

Jenny who saw it first. I heard her gasp. Then she was pointing at the floor.

From the door to the far wall there was a set of footprints. They weren't muddy marks. They were burnt into the wood. And they hadn't been made by shoes or boots.

The shape of hooves had been seared into the floorboards. They had been made by the Fiend.

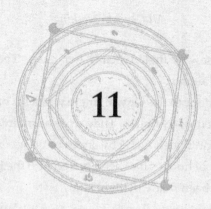

MY FATHER, THE FIEND

When the Fiend has a child by a witch, although exceptions happen, there are usually two likely outcomes. Either it's male and an abhuman or it's female – a daughter with the potential to wield strong magic.

My father was the Fiend – ain't any use pretending otherwise.

Ain't an abhuman, am I? So it's clear enough how I turned out. Bony Lizzie was my mam but I was brought up by foster parents and I didn't find out that truth for a long time. Lizzie trained me in witchcraft for two years but after that I was self-taught.

I could have ended up in one of the largest of the Pendle clans. Because although my second name is Deane, I'm really a Malkin. One thing saved me from that – meeting Tom Ward and becoming his friend. I helped him a lot, but the truth is that he helped me even more. My life began when I met Tom. I've said it before but I'll never stop repeating that because it's the truest thing I've ever said.

Our struggle against the Fiend lasted years, and one of the first times we ever saw signs that he walked the earth was his hoofprints burnt into floorboards as we'd just seen in that warehouse in Banks. I don't think Tom ever doubted my claim that I'd seen the Fiend on that ghost ship but now it was beyond dispute.

The Fiend was walking the earth once more.

Of course, that was a danger to us and the whole County but not yet as bad as it might be. No visitor from the dark can walk the earth during the hours of daylight. And, even after dark, any visit they make is short – usually a response to a summoning from a coven of witches. But if there was ever a large gathering of the witch clans, they could unite to enable the Fiend to walk the earth whenever he chose – even in daylight. The last time that had been attempted, the Fiend had been destroyed just in time to prevent that.

But now he was back and seemingly growing in power.

Me and Tom would certainly be his targets. He would want revenge and be eager to destroy us. I feared that we'd been lured to Banks for him to do just that. I still wanted to leave and go back to Chipenden and, once again, I suggested that to Tom but, as I'd expected, he refused.

We left the wharf and headed back, shocked by what we had seen. We didn't talk much. There was nothing much to be said. The whole County was in danger.

Once we reached Ralph's Wife's Lane, the girl asked Tom if he minded if she walked around the area for a while, rather than go straight back to the inn.

'Take care, Jenny, and don't stay away too long,' he warned her.

I asked myself why Jenny wanted to do that and it made me wonder about her even more. I was only too glad to get away. I would have expected her to feel the same way.

She set off down the lane in the opposite direction to the way back. But she didn't stay away that long, arriving back at the inn less than half an hour after us.

So now we had to lie in wait for the thing that had rapped upon the door and then gouged and burned it with its fiery talons.

Halloween was very close now and that always made me nervous. Being a witch myself I was only too aware how it made the dark and those who served it much stronger. The trouble was I didn't feel much stronger myself but I gathered my magic as best I could.

There wasn't much of it. I just hoped that it would be enough.

We could have split up, Tom and the girl watching from outside in the yard while I waited inside near the door. But Tom wouldn't hear of that. He wanted all three of us together, and so we were outside in the cold night air waiting close to the high stone wall that surrounded the yard. There was a double gate that led outside but that was barred and locked.

There was about five minutes to go before our unwelcome visitor was likely to arrive. Henry Jackson had said that the noises had begun exactly on the stroke of midnight.

The yard was empty but for four empty ale barrels arranged next to each other in a tidy line. It was a bright clear night with a moon that was less than two days short of full. The night was about as bright as it ever got in the County. Our view of the yard and door was perfect.

It was chilly but that was often the case during late autumn in the County. It might be pleasant enough during the day but, after dark, the temperature often dropped fast. It was getting really cold now and I was shivering so I was worried about Tom. Didn't want him catching a cold – it might turn into something worse.

The air had been perfectly calm and still, our breath steaming up into the cold air, when suddenly there was a change. There was a bestial roar from the sky directly above us and then we were being buffeted by a powerful wind that overturned two of the big wooden barrels and sent them rolling across the yard.

After that, everything happened very quickly. I sensed that something had joined us in the yard. Something invisible. There was no scratching and gouging at the back door. Instead of that, it was struck with a tremendous blow that broke the lock and sent it crashing back against the inside wall.

Then the thing was no longer invisible. It was at least eight feet tall and covered in a thick hide of fur. It was facing us, its long muscular arms raised above its head and long sharp talons extended. It could have been a huge bear but for two things.

Its face was hairless and human, with a wide mouth, a long bony nose and cruel narrow-set eyes. The second difference was its horns. They were not spiral ram's horns like those of the Fiend – these were long and sharp and jutted forward from its broad forehead. Those horns were deadly weapons that could kill with ease.

Then I heard the click of the retractable blade and Tom ran straight towards the creature, his staff pointing at its broad chest. It spun very quickly and grabbed the end of his staff and dragged it from Tom's grasp. As he staggered forward, losing his balance, the beast snapped the staff into two pieces and cast them away. Then it struck down towards Tom with the long sharp talons of its right hand.

Tom rolled away and just avoided those deadly talons and, my heart in my mouth at his narrow escape, I ran towards the creature. The closer I could get to it, the more effective my magic would be.

But there was another powerful gust of wind. It sent a barrel rolling directly into my path and I stumbled over it, just managing to use my hands to save my head from smashing on the cold hard flags.

I struggled to my feet, desperate to help Tom.

But help had arrived already.

Jenny ran straight at the beast even as it plunged its sharp talons towards Tom's throat. I was astonished at how fast she was moving.

Despite the failure of his attempt, Tom had attacked with the speed of a man half his age. Had the beast's reactions not been so quick, he would certainly have stabbed it with his silver-alloy blade.

But the girl was incredibly fast, her feet flying over the ground, and there was something graceful in the way she moved and wielded the weapon. It was almost as if she were dancing rather than running.

The blade of her staff entered the beast's left eye, going all the way in. It screamed as blood splashed into her face. She twisted the staff, withdrew it and stabbed the beast in the throat.

I was now on my feet, moving towards them, and I could see the expression on the girl's face. There was fierce concentration there and the kind of savage intent that you rarely saw on the face of a human. She withdrew the blade from the beast's throat and stabbed for a third time, towards its remaining eye.

The blade never made contact. There was another bestial roar and the beast vanished.

Once again the air was still and calm.

I walked over to Tom and helped him to his feet.

'You did well, Jenny,' I told the girl. 'You saved Tom.'

It was the first time that I'd called her by her name.

As we walked back into the inn, Henry Jackson came down the stairs, holding a lantern.

'Are you badly hurt, child?' he asked, staring at Jenny's blood-splattered face with a horrified expression.

Jenny grinned at him. 'It's not my blood,' she said. 'I stabbed it in the eye!'

'Looks like your apprentice did all the work,' Jackson said, looking at Tom, who was leaning against me heavily, carrying the two pieces of his broken staff in his left hand and limping a little.

'She did well,' Tom said.

'Indeed, and it's a good job that she did,' said the landlord. 'I suppose when you're long past your best years you need a good apprentice to do what's necessary.'

By now I was livid at the way Henry Jackson was showing no respect for Tom. I always try to avoid hitting back at people who don't know any better. But this time I just couldn't help myself. I used a spell – a little one that was usually very effective.

'I see you've had a little accident, Mr Jackson!' I told him, glancing down at the dark stain spreading across the front of his trousers. I watched his eyes widen with surprise and embarrassment, then pushed past him and led the way upstairs.

12

THE BALLAD OF JENNY CALDER

Back in our room I used the basin of water and a sponge and cleaned Jenny's face and hair as best I could. Then I sat next to Tom on the bed.

'You did really well, Jenny,' I told her. 'You were so very fast. I thought there was no way you could have reached Tom in time to save him. But you did.'

She shrugged. 'It's another of my gifts,' she said. 'It's just the way I am.'

The Jenny I had known many years earlier had already developed two gifts – there might have been more but, if so, she had concealed them. Firstly, she had been able to make herself almost invisible. It wasn't *true* invisibility but the knack of getting people not to notice you, which was just as good. Her second gift was that of empathy.

So if this was a third one, incredible speed, how many others were there?

'I don't think I destroyed it,' Jenny said. 'Do you think it'll come back?' She paused. 'Was it the same creature that was at Fletcher's Farm?'

Tom sighed. 'I'm reasonably sure it was the same – it attacked on different days, remember. But I think the real question is, will whoever sent it to this place send it again?'

'You mean the Fiend?' Jenny asked.

Tom shook his head. 'The Fiend can't visit the earth unless he's been summoned. Last night somebody must have summoned him – perhaps the same person or persons who called that beast to this yard. That's who we need to deal with.'

'Who could it be?' asked Jenny.

'As I said, that's the problem. Someone with powerful magic: a mage or a witch – most likely a whole coven of witches,' Tom said. 'But Alice is right – we're in real danger here. I no longer think of this as just another piece of spook's business. We've been lured here. We've taken the bait . . .'

What Tom had just said was the conclusion that I'd been moving towards very reluctantly. It was not a pleasant thought so I'd been in no rush to arrive at it.

'Could it be Henry Jackson?' Jenny asked. 'He was the one who sent for us.'

Tom didn't answer. He was gazing forlornly at the two pieces of his broken staff which he'd placed on the floor to the right of the door. It was his favourite staff. It had served him well for at least fifteen years. He had once had another one that he was extremely fond of too. But Wulf had borrowed it years ago and never returned it.

'It could be anyone,' I said. 'Just because Jackson is rude and obnoxious don't mean it has to be him. Anyway, Tom, you sound like you think it best to leave. That's what I've thought since yesterday and kept telling you.'

'Sorry, I should have listened to you earlier, Alice. We'll leave at first light. We need to be in Chipenden anyway, to go to Fletcher's Farm.'

After breakfast, we collected our belongings from our rooms and went looking for Henry Jackson. We found him in the kitchen talking to the cook who was scrubbing the breakfast pans.

'Ah, there you are, Mr Ward,' Jackson said. 'As I expected, you're running back home early with your tail between your legs.'

'We are not running anywhere!' Tom said angrily. 'We'll be back in less than a week to keep watch on your back door again – just in case that beast returns. But, as I said, there's nothing that I can do about the ghost in the lane. As for the ship, I need time to think about that and maybe ferret out information that might help. Anyway, I've come to pay what we owe for our accommodation . . .'

Henry Jackson held his hand up and shook his head. 'There'll be no charge for that. After all, your apprentice stopped that beast when it might well have entered the inn and done untold damage. As for any fee I might owe you, we'll leave that until you return and confirm the job is done. Is that fair enough, Mr Ward?'

'Yes, I'm happy with that. We'll be back within the week,' Tom said, turning away and leading the way to the front door of the inn.

'Yes, I'm sure you will,' Jackson called out to us as we left.

Danny was waiting outside and walked towards Jenny, arms wide as if to give her a hug. However, to my surprise, she scowled and walked right past him as if he wasn't there. Tom and I returned his nod and followed Jenny. I considered asking her what was wrong but thought better of it. It was her business after all.

The sun was shining out of a blue sky and my spirits were high. I was glad to see the back of Henry Jackson and the Black Bull. It wouldn't bother me if I never saw Churchtown again and Banks either. I resolved to try and talk Tom out of coming back but my fears of the previous night were gradually fading. Then, I'd felt certain that we'd been lured into a trap. Now I was not quite so sure.

Tom was carrying his broken staff, which he'd tried to repair by lashing the two halves together with string. Jenny was carrying his bag and she looked sad and a little angry. Perhaps she'd quarrelled with Danny?

We hadn't been walking more than half an hour when a mist began to form. Within a few minutes the sun was obscured and we couldn't see more than a few feet ahead of us. But Tom carried on leading the way, about ten paces ahead. He was just a faint shape in the fog, showing not the slightest hint of hesitation.

I could hear the crashing of waves to our left. The tide would be going out by now, slowly retreating across the marsh back towards the Ribble estuary. Somewhere to our right, as we headed east, would be Martin Mere. We were on the track between the sea marsh and the lake with its surrounding bog. Soon enough we were ankle deep in mud, horrible black clingy stuff.

I cheered myself up with the thought that another half hour or so would see us clear of it and walking on firmer ground. But that didn't happen. Tom had come to a halt and waves were licking at his boots. When we came abreast of him, I could see larger waves moving with force from the left, barring our path.

For a moment I thought that Tom might have become disorientated and led us towards the estuary. But we were still on the track, that was clear enough, and it led towards water, waves that shouldn't have been there.

'The tide should be ebbing, not continuing to rise,' Tom said. 'We'll have to wait until it subsides . . .'

It wasn't a pleasant wait. There was nowhere to sit down and we had to keep on our feet. The air was chilly and damp and it wasn't really worth pacing around because of the clingy mud.

But we had to move soon enough because suddenly I could hear water behind us too. Lucky it was that we went to take a look, otherwise we'd have drowned for sure. Waves were surging in from the estuary, cutting off our retreat, and we had to go through them or we'd have been cut off and trapped. Even so, at one point the water was well above our knees, the waves buffeting us so hard that it was difficult to keep on our feet.

Drenched and bedraggled, we got through somehow. But we were exhausted. I was worried about Tom catching a chill that might turn into something worse so I suggested heading back towards Churchtown. Both Tom and Jenny agreed quickly and as we walked it soon became apparent that we had no choice but to return to the Black Bull.

When we reached it, the mist was already clearing but a light drizzle was drifting in from the north.

Henry Jackson was waiting at the front door, his arms folded and a grin on his face. 'Didn't expect you back *quite* so soon!' he said. 'Will you be wanting overnight accommodation again?'

Tom nodded. 'I thought the tide should have been ebbing,' he told Jackson. 'But the path ahead was deep under water and we almost got cut off.'

'We get freak tides here – happens at least once a year. They are totally unpredictable. If I'd had the slightest inkling I'd have warned you, Mr Ward. But not to worry. Come inside and get yourselves dry. My advice is to rest up, have another night here – on the house, may I add – and set off for home tomorrow. What do you say?'

'That's kind of you, Mr Jackson,' Tom said.

I wasn't going to argue so we returned to the same rooms and stayed there until it was time to go down to supper. But I was far from happy at what had occurred. It almost seemed as if events were conspiring to force us to stay in the area.

We sat at our usual table and ate our supper. This time it was a big portion of steaming hotpot and it was so tasty that I could have eaten twice as much.

The usual bunch of fishermen were there in their working clothes, some of them leaning on the bar, others chatting boisterously in groups of two or three. As we finished our meal, Danny came into the room carrying his guitar and took up his usual position in front of the curtained window.

He strummed a single chord to signal that he was about to begin and the room immediately fell silent.

'I've written another song,' Danny announced. 'This is dedicated to the pretty lady sitting over there!' he said, gesturing towards us.

Well, he certainly didn't mean me, and as everyone in the room glanced towards us, the pretty lady in question was blushing pink but she wasn't smiling.

'The title of my new song is "The Ballad of Jenny Calder",' Danny said. He strummed an introduction and then he began to sing, his voice deeper and even more melodic than last time. He seemed to get better each time he sang.

'A girl can't be an apprentice
A girl can't become a spook
A girl can't stand against the dark
Here's a saucepan – become a cook!

A girl can't bind a boggart
A girl can't fight a witch
A girl can't stand against the dark
Be a seamstress – learn to stitch!'

Everyone in the room was male but for me and Jenny. Loud laughter and whistles of approval greeted the first two verses. I thought it clear enough that their mirth was due to the advice given to any girl, since girls were not fit to be a spook. But the tone of the third verse was different and my anger and the laughter began to die away.

> 'But I'm my mother's seventh daughter
> And she was a seventh too
> I can stand against the dark
> Just show me what to do
>
> "Be an obedient wife!" laughed Spook Johnson
> "Learn how to butter bread!"
> Spook Brinscall had less to say
> He set his dogs on her instead
>
> Tom Ward was somewhat kinder
> But he refused her too
> But in good time he changed his mind
> And his respect for her, it grew
>
> My name is Jenny Calder
> I'll be the very first female spook
> I'm working hard
> To learn my trade
> And the boggart is the cook!'

There was applause and the stamping of feet in response to the ballad that young Danny had written and performed. Despite the opening lines, it was a tribute to Jenny's perseverance. I thought she would be pleased. But when I glanced towards her, Jenny was already coming to her feet and the blush had given way to the whiteness of anger. Her eyes blazing with fury, she left the room without even a glance towards Danny.

'That song upset her,' I told Tom. 'I'll go up and see what's wrong.'

'Then I'll come up with you,' Tom said. 'I feel tired and just a bit shivery. But don't worry, Alice, a good night's sleep will put me right.'

I hoped that Tom wasn't coming down with something nasty. After his illness, he was vulnerable to infections. What might be nothing more than a cold for me could make him take to his bed for days.

Jenny was in her room and it took quite a bit of knocking before she finally came to the door. Her eyes were red and swollen. She'd obviously been crying.

'Come back to our room for a while, Jenny,' I told her. 'We need to talk.'

Once there, she began to sob so I sat her on the bed next to me and put my arm across her shoulder in an attempt to comfort her. Tom took the chair opposite.

'What's wrong?' I asked. 'Was it the song that upset you? I don't think Danny meant it to hurt you.'

'Yes, it was the song,' Jenny said. 'And I do think he meant to hurt and mock me. It told me that Danny is not who he pretends to be. Now he scares me. There were things in that ballad that I never told him.'

'Such as?' Tom asked.

'He said the boggart was the cook. I never told him that!'

'I wouldn't worry about that,' Tom said. 'Lots of folk have visited that Chipenden house over the years and lots of apprentices lived there, especially in John Gregory's time. Some went on to become spooks while some just ran away and turned to other trades. People talk – it's natural. By now it could be common knowledge that the Chipenden spook has a boggart guarding the house and garden and that it also makes the breakfasts.'

Jenny shook her head. 'There's more to it than that. How did he know that Judd Brinscall set his dogs on me? You and Alice are the only people who know about that and Judd is dead. How did he know that Spook Johnson had rejected me too? That was over forty years ago!'

Desperate to be taken on as a spook's apprentice, Jenny had asked both Johnson and Brinscall to train her and both had rejected her.

'I just thought you'd told him those things and so he'd put them into his song,' Tom said.

'Well, I didn't!' Jenny said, almost snapping at Tom. 'He either plucked them from my mind or used some kind of dark magic to learn about my past! And do you know something else? He's a liar too. And I hate liars! I took a walk yesterday afternoon to get a look at the house where he said his mother lived. But there was only the ruin of a cottage at the end of the lane! He'd tricked me. This whole place is creepy and so are the people who live here. I just hope that we can get away tomorrow.'

I agreed with Jenny. My sense of danger was growing again.

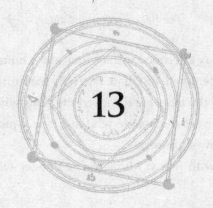

13

MIRROR WRITING

The next morning we set off for Chipenden right after breakfast. Danny wasn't outside to say goodbye, which was a relief. I didn't like to think how Jenny would react if she saw him.

Once again, the sun was shining but it wasn't long before a mist began to form. Soon the visibility was even worse than the previous day. After about ten minutes you could hardly see your hand in front of your face.

The ground was just as boggy underfoot as more rain had fallen overnight and soon it got worse as we reached the place where we'd almost been cut off by the tide and drowned. At least there wasn't that to worry about. I could hear the sea on our left but the sound of the waves was faint and the tide was a long way out.

We walked for about an hour and I gradually realized that we wouldn't be going home this day either. The sound of the sea was now even fainter but it was puzzling me. It seemed to be coming from our right, not our left. Then the mist lifted and the air was clear but there were very low clouds. We could see something that we didn't want to see.

Directly ahead of us was Churchtown, the sharp spire of the abandoned church spearing the clouds. We were right back where we'd started.

'We're being prevented from leaving by some kind of spell, Alice,' Tom said. 'Can you do anything about it?'

We came to a halt. I closed my eyes and concentrated. There was one dark spell I knew that caused confusion in the victim's mind. It made you wander in circles, bewildered and lost. I might have been able to do something about that. But the other possibility was a spell so powerful that it could affect the weather and tides – even distort paths and make a journey from one place to another impossible.

I tried to feel what it was, then sensed the magic and recoiled. It was the second type, a spell so powerful that even at my strongest I would have had no guarantee of being able to cast it with any hope of success. And there was certainly no way I could counter it.

'It's too strong. I can't help. Only one of the Old Gods can work such a powerful spell.'

'You mean the Fiend?' Tom asked.

'It's more than likely. Either the Fiend himself or someone drawing directly upon his power.'

'Right, then let's try another route,' Tom said. 'We'll head towards Ormskirk.'

Ormskirk wasn't the fastest route back to Chipenden but any path that led us away from Churchtown was fine by me.

This time the way wasn't boggy. The going was good with a much firmer track. But we still had the mist to contend with, which closed in again within ten minutes of setting off. We were heading inland so there was no warning from the sea either, no hint that we were no longer going in the right direction. I really began to believe that we would escape the spell.

But within less than an hour the mist cleared very suddenly and directly ahead of us was Churchtown, the narrow pointy spire rising above the dwellings.

Tom shrugged and we trudged towards it, the weather changing again as we walked. The force of the wind was increasing and darker clouds were sweeping in from the estuary, the gloom deepening with every step.

Henry Jackson was waiting for us outside the Black Bull and he wasn't alone. As he walked towards us, the fishermen were at his back. There were over a dozen of them. I heard footsteps, glanced behind and saw others closing in.

'I can offer you another night of hospitality!' Jackson called out. 'But this time I'm afraid it won't be quite so comfortable.'

Then I felt a tremendous blow to the back of my head and I fell into darkness.

Tough as old boots, I am. But they'd hit me with something at least as hard as my skull. I woke up with a bad headache and I was on my back, unable to move.

One glance told me why. I had been bound with Tom's silver chain. It stretched from my shoulders down to my knees, binding my arms and legs together. To bind me properly it needed more of what spooks called 'spread' and the chain should have extended further upwards to bind my mouth and stop me casting spells that needed words. Probably they believed that I was past it and not particularly powerful.

They were both right and wrong. Although my magic was depleted I could still have my moments. As I said, being old means that others sometimes underestimate what you're capable of and that can be a good thing but can also sometimes be annoying. One short-sighted farmer once offered to help me up a flight of steps. I could have run up them faster than he could, but I didn't take offence and refused politely.

The silver-alloy chain didn't cause me any pain as long as I kept still – all my life I'd had some resistance to silver, more than most witches – but it would be hard to get free from it. Gritting my teeth, I came up onto my knees and saw that I was in some sort of storeroom. It was full of packing cases and junk but also contained some large barrels of ale. That suggested that I was somewhere inside the Black Bull. The floor was wooden boards rather than flags, so I wasn't at ground level.

There was a sturdy oaken door, no doubt locked, and one narrow window with vertical bars and no glass. No doubt the bars were to stop thirsty locals from climbing the outside wall and carrying away the barrels. It was pitch black outside, probably the middle of the night, and everything was silent. There were no sounds coming from within the building either. I was now convinced that this was the inn.

I started worrying about Tom. There was cold air coming in through the window and it was chilly. If he was held in a similar room to this, the chill was sure to get into his chest. Then I thought of Jenny and felt sorry for her too. Unless I could do something about our situation, I guessed that her apprenticeship and her life would be short like her previous one.

I could have dragged myself to the window to see what was outside. Or maybe got to the door to see if I could budge it. But the chain binding me made that difficult. It would have required a lot of effort. So I decided to save my strength for daylight. I lay back and forced myself to sleep but using just a little nudge of magic to ensure that I awoke just before dawn.

*

I awoke as I'd planned and rolled myself over and over until I reached the wall directly under the narrow window. It hurt but I forced myself to my feet and peered outside.

I could see the church and the village green below and judged that I was being held in one of the inn's first-floor storerooms. Nobody was in sight but there was something at the centre of the green that immediately caught my eye.

It was a huge stack of wood and kindling. Had I been a prisoner of the Church I would have presumed that a bonfire had been built to burn me. But the church was locked and abandoned. There was no priest or Quisitor in Churchtown.

So what was the fire for?

Perhaps the blow to my head meant that I wasn't thinking clearly. Otherwise, I'd have guessed the truth within minutes. But it was almost an hour later when it finally dawned on me. I suppose it was the arrival of a group of women. There were thirteen of them and one sniff told me that they were witches although none that I recognized. But they were a coven all right. They halted and stared towards the pile of wood as if they wanted it to burst into flames as soon as possible.

Then there was something else that confirmed it. I knew that today was the 31st of October, one of the four main witches' sabbaths – *Halloween*.

They were going to summon the Fiend who would arrive in the midst of the flames at midnight. The coven would make obeisance, bowing and grovelling before him to acknowledge his superiority. In return, he would grant them some power. That was what usually happened, but I suspected that tonight would be different.

We would be given to the Fiend. We would join him in the flames.

As I watched, another group of witches arrived. They were not from the Pendle clans and their garb told me that they were from another county far to the south.

They were Essex witches.

I sat down with my back to the window and thought things through. All those years ago, when I'd helped Tom to destroy the Fiend, we'd lured him to the earth and with the help of Old Gregory and Grimalkin had staked him in a pit then cut his head from his huge body. Grimalkin had kept the Fiend's head in a sack and fought alone to keep it from the hands of our enemies so they couldn't rejoin the two pieces.

Although some Pendle witches had been involved, most of the enemies who opposed us had been from Essex.

The Old Gods could return if enough people worship them. This is what must have happened. Down in Essex, the witch clans through faith, magic and dark wishes had returned the Fiend to awareness and would now be helping him to regain his power.

No surprise then that his supporters had sought to lure us to this place where he could pay back Tom and me for what we'd done. Henry Jackson had been carrying out the Fiend's wishes.

Old Gregory was beyond his reach – he'd died at the Battle of Wardstone – but what about Grimalkin, the witch assassin? Had he already dealt with her in the dark?

Really brave she was, Grimalkin, as well as a fierce fighter. She had hated the Fiend since her childhood, disliking the ways he controlled her clan. She didn't want him anywhere near her. But to achieve that, a sacrifice was necessary. If a witch had a child by the Fiend then, unless she willed it, he could never approach her again. So that was what she did. After the birth, he was allowed to visit the mother just one more time to inspect his offspring.

But Grimalkin had given birth to a perfectly normal human child, a baby boy, and she'd loved that helpless tiny dependent creature. She loved being a mother to it. To her surprise and horror, the Fiend had lifted Grimalkin's child and dashed its head against a rock, killing it instantly.

From that moment she had striven to destroy the Fiend.

The first time she'd managed to harm him, her first sweet taste of revenge, had been at a witches' sabbath where the Deane clan had prepared a huge fire to tempt the Fiend into their presence. Grimalkin hid and watched from afar as the thirteen members of the Deane coven joined hands and formed a circle round the fire.

At midnight, the flames changed from orange to red and the Fiend materialized at the very centre of the bonfire. His body was covered with thick black hair and he had huge ram's horns and a long tail. He could change his size and was three times the size of a human male – made himself big to impress the Deanes, he had. But that was a big mistake because it gave Grimalkin an easier target. She had forged three silver-tipped blades and now she dared what none before her had ever attempted.

Grimalkin attacked the Fiend.

When she was close enough, she threw the first blade at her target, striking the Fiend in the chest. Her second two blades were not thrown as successfully, but they still buried themselves in that hairy body. The Fiend screamed with pain, but as she got closer he was forced to vanish as even he could not defy the rule that said he could not approach anyone who had borne his child unless she wished it.

The Deanes were shocked and in disarray, allowing Grimalkin to flee back into the darkness. They sent three assassins after her but she killed them all.

After that, Grimalkin trained hard, sharpening her fighting skills, and eventually killed Kernolde, the Malkin witch assassin, and took her place.

Grimalkin was dead now but she had the power to leave the dark, only not during the daylight hours. Since her death, on more than one occasion she had helped me and Tom destroy our common enemies. But she had not replied to me for many long years.

Now, however, I was desperate and decided to try once more.

A witch can communicate using a mirror. Once the link has been established in the past, all that is necessary is to breathe upon it and write a message to the person you wish to contact.

I'd noticed a fragment of broken glass by the door. It was small, no larger than half the size of my palm, but it was reflective, positioned as it was upon the dirty floor. It would suffice. I was very adept, having practised such skills for most of my long life. I could even communicate using the surface of water.

I rolled towards the shard of glass, positioned my face above it and breathed upon its surface so that it became clouded. My arms were still bound to my side with the chain, so I was forced to write the message to the witch assassin with the tip of my tongue. It was a difficult thing to do but I persevered.

The glass cleared but I could not see the face of Grimalkin. I breathed upon the glass again and tried once more. There was no need to tell her our whereabouts. If she was alive, she could find us with ease.

> Grimalkin,
>
> This is Alice. Tom and I are in mortal danger. The Fiend
> has returned and is being summoned this very night.
> Unless you can help, we will be sacrificed to him.
>
> Alice

I waited. But there was no reply. No sight of Grimalkin's face. No reply drawn upon the glass. I tried for a third time but then gave up.

There could be only one reason for Grimalkin not replying.

She must have been destroyed.

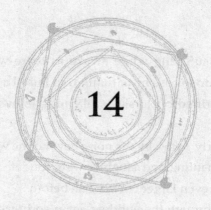

14

POOR TOM

I was filled with despair and lay upon my back and closed my eyes. I tried to sleep but failed, and eventually I heard noises from outside, shrieking and chanting. So, still bound by the silver chain, I rolled myself towards the barred window once more.

After a struggle, I got up onto my feet again and peered down at the village green. More witches had arrived – about a hundred or so. That meant eight or nine covens in all. This was more than just a small gathering to offer us to the Fiend.

Were they trying what the Pendle witches had attempted all those long years ago? Did they intend to bring the Fiend fully into our world so that he could walk the earth?

No doubt tonight we would find out. Once again, I worried about Tom and Jenny. My captors brought me no food or water and my mouth was parched. There was no point in suffering while awake as there was nothing that I could do to ease my situation, so I used a little magic again and drifted off to sleep, planning to awaken in the afternoon.

Woken early, I was, by the noise beyond the window. The shrieking, chanting and laughter were louder. The volume indicated an even larger crowd than before.

I looked through the window again and was astonished at just how many people had gathered on the green. There must have been over thirty covens of witches and among them some men. They had gathered in groups. The bonfire at the centre looked bigger than ever. They'd probably added more wood.

This was a big enterprise. My suspicion was beyond doubt now. This would be no fleeting sabbath visit by the Fiend.

They were going to celebrate Halloween by enabling him to walk the earth.

A new age of darkness would begin.

I had one last hope – one that I would use with great reluctance and only as a last resort.

I would try to summon Wulf.

I blame myself for what happened between me, my daughter and Wulf. I was the one who turned things bad. At first, I'd really liked the boy and he'd once played an important part in saving my life – and Tom's too. I could forgive a lot when somebody did that.

But Wulf changed. It wasn't his fault. He had been slain by a servant of the evil goddess Circe. But that was not the end of him. At the time he was being trained as a tulpar by his new master, Hrothgar, coached to create tulpas, entities that were thoughts made flesh and could have an independent life of their own. But Wulf was extremely talented and some of the wraith tulpas that he'd created became new bodies for him to inhabit after his natural body had been buried. For Wulf, after early difficulties, it eventually became as easy as drawing on a garment.

One tulpa was in the shape of a fanged wolf-beast with wings. Another was identical to the body that had died. And although she was young, I knew my daughter, Tilda, was in love with him, despite the fact that Wulf was no longer human.

Tilda first went off with Wulf in order to visit Wulf's previous master, Spook Johnson, and fight the Pendle witches. I tried to persuade her not to go but I didn't use magic or any other means to prevent her leaving. Ain't even sure I could have stopped her if I'd tried. Tilda had a strong will. Not only that, she had Tom's blood and mine running through her veins and was already a powerful witch.

My powers were beginning their slow decline just as Tilda's were starting to grow.

*

When they returned a few months later, quietly pleased about the results they had achieved – the power of the Pendle witches had been severely diminished – we began to really quarrel: mother and daughter exchanging more hateful words than friendly ones. Wulf tried to keep out of our fights but if forced to choose sides he naturally took Tilda's. It even caused problems between me and Tom. He tried to keep out of it too but, when we were alone, he would plead for me to be more tolerant.

Eventually, Wulf and Tilda left again, a cloud of anger covering the three of us, Tom keeping his distance, scything the grass so that he need not be part of it.

But they did not return. It was as if they had disappeared from the face of the earth. I was hurt that they never even tried to contact me and Tom. How could my own daughter do that?

I had not seen them since. Almost thirty years had passed and my bitterness had grown. In my mind I no longer had a daughter.

But, although my pride had kept me from attempting it before, I did have the means of reaching them. I'd once given Wulf a mirror, telling him that, if he were ever in danger, he could contact me and I would come to his aid. Whether or not he still had the mirror did not matter. Any reflective surface near Wulf would do, once the link had been made.

Little did I guess that I would be the one to need *his* help.

I breathed upon the glass and, as before, wrote a short message on that clouded surface with the tip of my tongue.

Wulf

Tom and I are in grave danger. We are the captives of a large gathering of covens who plan to raise the Fiend this very night. We are in Churchtown, which is on the southern bank of the Ribble estuary.

Alice

I didn't refer to Jenny. Wulf had never met her, although Tom might have mentioned her to him. But, as I wrote the message, I did not see Wulf's face gazing back at me.

I waited but there was no reply written upon the glass. I had believed that, despite my differences with Tilda, if possible Wulf would try to help. But now my sudden fear was that both he and my daughter had been slain or were held captive somewhere. Otherwise, I could not believe she would be so cruel as to refuse my plea for help?

One possibility was that they'd journeyed to some distant land – somewhere too far away even for Wulf to reach us in time. But in that case he would at least reply.

I had tried my best. I'd tried and failed to contact Grimalkin. Then I'd swallowed my pride and tried to contact Wulf. Neither had answered.

There was just one more thing that I could do.

It was more difficult and rarely used. I could do it although it would deplete more of my small reserve of magic. But what choice did I have?

So I cast the spell, draining myself further. Now, whenever Wulf next came face to face with a reflective surface, whether a mirror or even a puddle or a basin of water, he'd see that message, my plea for help, written there.

I just hoped that he would see it in time.

I had visitors.

The door opened and Henry Jackson walked in with young Danny.

The innkeeper was dapper as usual, wearing a spotless white shirt, dark trousers and shoes so highly polished that, as he walked towards me, I could see my face reflected in them. Danny was dressed as usual too, in fisherman's clothes, and had the same wide smile on his face that he had often used when greeting Jenny.

Jackson gave me a sharp poke in my ribs with his toecap. 'Look at me, witch! Look at me when I'm speaking to you!

'It's time to pay you exactly what you deserve!' he continued. 'For years you've inflicted damage upon those we serve and got away with it. Did you think you could escape punishment forever? Spook Ward deserves his comeuppance too and we'll give him as painful a death as possible. And we'll snuff out that brat of a girl before she becomes another thorn in our side. For *you* and the girl there'll be something special. Your souls will go straight to the dark. Those waiting for you will know exactly what to do!'

I was filled with a great sadness at that. I feared the torments waiting for me. But, far worse than that, I dreaded what had cast a shadow over much of my life with Tom. We'd shared happiness on earth but death would tear us apart. Tom had done good things all his life and so, despite his lamia blood, would surely go to the light, whereas I was doomed to go to the dark. Tom and I would be separated without hope of ever seeing each other again.

It was then that Danny moved closer and stood over me. As he did so, his handsome face began to change. What had been visible before had been conjured by *glamour* – a powerful spell of illusion.

Now I saw him for what he truly was. Instead of skin his narrow face was covered in dark blue scales and he had three eyes, one of them twice as large as the other two and set in the centre of his forehead. It was the demon that I'd seen on the ghost ship standing close to the Fiend.

'Well, old witch,' said Jackson, 'you might well look upon my companion with astonishment and fear. He is a prince of the dark, no less, and he is related to you! This is a favourite son of the Fiend whose growing strength has played a major part in restoring his father to power once more.'

Having visited me briefly with no other purpose than to gloat and increase my fear, they then left me alone with my thoughts. There were many mysteries here. I'd not known of the existence of that son of the Fiend. Witches or abhumans were, of course, the usual offspring of the Fiend and a witch. But there were exceptions. Grimalkin's baby son had been a perfect human and that was why the Fiend had slain the child. But no doubt there were other children of the Fiend who were different – like that three-eyed demon. And maybe his mother hadn't been a witch?

Perhaps she'd been a goddess from the dark like Circe?

And what had been said about Jenny was another mystery. What had she done that made them so certain that she would go to the dark rather than the light? She'd spent time with that demon who'd been in the form of the handsome young Danny. Could that deception have damned her? Or was it something else? It was one more mystery to solve.

More than once I went to the window and peered down upon the green. Each time more witches had gathered. There was a lot of shouting and screeching. I looked towards the huge stack of wood and saw a dirty little mongrel dog peeing on the edge of it. That made me smile. It was like piddling on the Fiend's throne, but a witch aimed a kick at it and the creature moved away.

After dark I kept away. But about eleven I heard the crackle of burning wood and saw sparks shoot up into the sky.

It was approaching midnight when they came for me. Henry Jackson was there, a smirk on his face. He kept his distance and let two of the burly fishermen do his dirty work. Of the three-eyed demon there was no sign.

One stuffed a ball of dirty cloth into my mouth and tied it in place with a double loop of rope round my face. I couldn't believe it was to prevent me from uttering spells because some of the witches would have sniffed out my magic and known that it was weak. The gag might just have been to prevent me from giving them a piece of my mind.

I would have told them what for too. There was no way that I'd choose to go to my death quietly.

Then they pushed me downstairs and dragged me through the front doorway of the inn and to the edge of the green. It was chaos with witches screaming, shouting and dancing with abandon. Above there was a full moon casting its yellow light upon the green. The bonfire had already been lit and was ablaze, the sky above it illuminated with sparks. Some of the witches tried to spit in my face as the fishermen dragged me through the throng towards the edge of the fire, my pointy shoes trailing on the grass.

There they pulled me upright and my heart sank as I saw poor Tom. He'd been badly beaten. One of his eyes was almost closed, there were lumps on his forehead and his hair was streaked with blood.

Once, because of the lamia blood that he'd inherited from his mam, they would have paid a terrible price for such violence. When his life was threatened, Tom had been able to transform into a creature that was part-human, part-lamia. With the strength and ferocity that brought, he would have slain his captors with ease and freed us within minutes. But that ability had declined with age just as my magic had slowly weakened. It was many years since Tom's lamia blood had last transformed him and I had no hope of that happening now.

Then I glimpsed Jenny, her face illuminated by the firelight. Her eyes were swollen with tears. There were no swellings on her face but it had been scratched by fingernails, five bloody lines gouged deeply into her right cheek. That wound was certain to leave scars. Not that it mattered now. She didn't have much of a future to look forward to. And if Jackson had been right, once in the dark, both of us would face something far worse than a painful death.

Neither Jenny nor Tom was bound. Again, their captors probably didn't consider them a threat as they hardly had the strength to stay on their feet.

Tom tried to speak to me, no doubt words of reassurance, but I couldn't hear what he said because of the uproar surrounding us. But gradually the spontaneous manic cries began to subside and the witches began to chant in unison. Midnight was approaching and they were begging the Fiend to appear.

No doubt when he did, we'd be pushed into the flames as an offering. I found it hard to accept that, after all we'd been through, our lives were going to end like this.

The chanting slowly fell into chaos as individual witches began to curse their enemies. They were using this moment to draw upon the dark power unleashed by the Fiend's expected arrival.

The yellow flames changed to orange and then to red, and the witches gathered in anticipation. I shuddered with a mixture of anger and fear as the Fiend began to materialize. He was anything if not predictable. As usual he chose his most intimidating form. At least three times the size of a man, he was, the flames reaching no higher than his knees. Curved ram's horns adorned his huge head and a long sinuous hairy tail snaked behind him. His whole body was covered in a thick black hide and his eyes were like burning coals and he seemed to be staring directly at me.

Our captors seized us then and began to push us towards the fire.

Tom groaned and Jenny began to scream.

I struggled desperately but it was a waste of time. My strength was all but gone. I could feel the fierce heat of the fire on my face. Within moments my skin would start to blister. It was over for me. I was an old woman who would soon flicker into flame, my dry flesh and bones becoming burnt dust to be scattered on the wind.

But I felt no pity for myself. All I could think about was poor Tom. All his life he'd fought the dark.

The last spook didn't deserve for it to end this way.

WULF'S TALE

Nearly thirty years earlier

15

THE MYSTERIOUS LOCKED DOOR

'You have no respect for me and your father, Tilda. If you had, you'd do as I ask – not leave again against my wishes!'

I was in the Chipenden garden but their voices had been loud enough to carry outdoors. In the distance I could see Tom Ward scything the grass. He didn't look towards me. I knew that he found the quarrels between Tilda and her mother as difficult as I did. We both tried not to interfere. I thought Alice and Tilda needed to be calmer and listen to each other more; I'd tried telling Tilda that but it made no difference.

However, I could not deny that what Alice demanded was something that both Tilda and I didn't wish to agree to. She thought Tilda was too young to be such close friends with me and didn't like us spending so much time together.

She'd had enough of our adventures, and wanted Tilda to stay at home for at least another year. As for me – I was supposed to leave the Chipenden house without Tilda and carry on my studies with Hrothgar. In addition to advancing my training as a tulpar, these studies would help us in our fight against the dark. We had clipped the claws of the Pendle witches, but they would surely regroup . . . As would others.

I listened for Tilda's reply but there was just the sound of a door being slammed somewhere in the house and then Tilda came out into the garden, her face red with anger. She marched towards her father at a furious pace. I followed at her heels.

'I take it that means you're going with Wulf!' Tom said, giving Tilda a hug. Then he patted me on the shoulder. 'Take care, both of you! Look after each other!'

We both nodded. 'A few weeks and we'll be back to visit you,' Tilda said, and then led the way out of the garden and away from Chipenden.

We walked back to Hrothgar's underworld in silence. Neither one of us was happy. I was angry with Tilda because I thought that she and her mother were equally to blame for the exchange of harsh words. Why did they have to part like that? So we didn't speak on the journey.

When we reached the edge of Hrothgar's lair, we prepared to leave the County. Approaching its secret entrance marked by two tall sycamore trees, I glanced towards the cottage close by. I glimpsed a face peering through a gap in the lace curtains. It was Mother Martha, a tulpa servant who was Hrothgar's link with the outside world. She usually did the shopping in the village.

As we walked between the twin sycamores, everything changed. Gone were the dark grey clouds blustering in from the west, to be replaced by the red sky of the underworld. The wind which had been buffeting my whole body and threatening to tear the hood from my head was replaced by calm still air.

We strode quickly through the trees, fearing the huge beasts that guarded this domain. Hrothgar had promised that we'd be safe but on each return I was always tense and nervous despite that. Circumstances could change.

But I needn't have been concerned. There were growls, rumblings and the distant thud of heavy feet but nothing moved towards us and soon I could glimpse the imposing mansion through a gap in the trees.

Once more I was gazing at the large country house, the grand dwelling of Hrothgar, surrounded by an ornamental moat over which a small bridge arched, leading to an extensive sunken lawn. Beyond that, stone steps led up to the house. It was extremely wide and double-fronted with mullioned windows and two rows of windows that suggested that the impressive dwelling had two storeys.

But, of course, there was only one floor. Hrothgar was a giant and, when standing on that single ground floor of the house, his eyes would be level with the upper row of windows.

As we crossed the bridge, Tilda suddenly gripped my hand and squeezed it. I squeezed back. With that gesture I knew we had forgiven each other. Our quarrels never lasted very long.

'Stopped sulking, have you?' Tilda asked, smiling at me.

'Yes, no more sulks!' I said, smiling back warmly.

We walked along the raised path that divided the sunken lawn and began to climb the steps. There were a lot of them – well over a hundred – until at last we came to the front door of the mansion, which was exactly as I remembered it – wooden, ornately carved and highly polished but designed to accommodate Hrothgar. It had the usual width of a human door but was over twice the expected height, extending upwards as far as the upper floor windows.

I raised my right hand and bunched it into a fist ready to knock. But before I could do so, the door opened and the tall thin giant was framed in the doorway, looking down at me.

No thinner than an average human man, he was almost twice as tall, thus creating that appearance of a skinny body. From head to toe, Hrothgar was over eleven feet tall, his clothing similar to that of a spook with a long black gown and a hood. His hands were noticeably large too, at least twice the normal human span.

His face was human, the eyes bright and intelligent, the nose hooked like an eagle's beak, which gave him a slightly cruel predatory appearance.

Of course, both Hrothgar and I were no longer human. Although born of human mothers our original bodies were dead and our souls now inhabited the tulpas which we had created. But there was no way to detect that from our appearance.

For a moment he did not acknowledge us and I feared that we might be unwelcome. Then his face was transformed with a broad smile and he leaned down and clapped me on both shoulders. 'Welcome, Wulf!' he cried. 'Welcome, Tilda!'

Standing aside, he then waved us inside.

He showed us to the same bedrooms where we had stayed previously and left us. He went with a smile and bade us to join him when we were ready. 'You are just in time for supper. We will meet in the dining room,' he said as he left me at the door of my room.

I pulled off my boots so as not to muddy any of the three white lambswool rugs or mark the polished wooden floor. Then I washed my face and hands using the bowl of water left for me on the table. The room had been prepared so Hrothgar must have been expecting us. No doubt he had taken on some form that could fly and had spied us from afar earlier in the day.

Tilda and I walked down to the dining room together. The door was wide open. I rapped on it out of politeness and Hrothgar beckoned us to join him. This was the place where we used to dine together during our previous times spent in this house of many rooms. It contained two tables and three chairs. One combination was suited to the average human and that was where we were to sit.

The other, the much larger table and chair, was built for the thin giant. Each table was furnished with white plates, Hrothgar's twice the size as ours, with knives and forks surrounded by dishes of steaming fish and vegetables. I knew that all this had been provided by his tulpa servants.

'Help yourselves,' Hrothgar said. 'We will speak when our appetites are satisfied.'

That was something else that I remembered about him. He rarely ate and spoke at the same time. Food demanded his total attention.

So we helped ourselves to fillets of trout, buttered potatoes, butter beans and carrots. When we'd finished dining, he rose to his feet and beckoned us to follow him.

'We will retire to the library and discuss what lies ahead,' he said.

Tilda and I had both spent lots of time in that library but now we noticed that one thing had changed. There were still the high library shelves stacked with books and the moveable ladders needed to access them. There were also the chairs and the table where Tilda and I had sat and studied together. But there was a new piece of furniture – a large padded reclining chair directly beneath the two vertically positioned windows, and it was of the perfect size to accommodate Hrothgar. It was upholstered in black leather with a matching footstool and the thin giant made himself comfortable there while we took our seats at the table.

Then I noticed something else. Tom Ward's staff was still leaning against the wall where I had left it months earlier, before leaving the house with Tilda to continue our adventures and eventually visit Tom and Alice again. I'd meant to return that staff to its owner, but it kept slipping my mind. Not that the need was urgent. Tom had spare staffs.

'When you leave you may return that to Spook Ward,' Hrothgar said, gesturing towards the staff.

Something in his tone suggested to me that he anticipated that I would carry it away sooner rather than later. He had never mentioned it during our previous visits here.

'Have I arrived at an inconvenient time?' I asked.

'I will not lie to you out of politeness, Wulf. I have some difficult and urgent problems to solve and, initially, I will not be able to devote to you all the attention that you deserve,' he explained. 'But we will manage as best we can so do not consider for a single moment that you are not welcome. But, for a while, you two will have to work and study mostly alone. Then, when my task is completed, Wulf, I will continue to augment your training as before. Is there anything you could work at until I am free?' he asked. 'It will take me a week or so at the most . . .'

'Yes, and it's something that I've been thinking of doing for a while but, apart from one creation, I never did anything about it. Perhaps now's the time to finally get on with it. My number of bound tulpas is limited. I would like to begin by developing more of them.'

Hrothgar nodded. 'How many bound tulpas can you inhabit at present?' he asked.

I had the human body that I wore now, which was a copy of the flesh that I was born into. Then there was the sky wolf, also Raphael who was a winged angel and Saint Quentin who had the skill of opening locks. My one new addition to that was a slightly older and larger warrior version of myself complete with mail armour and weapons – I called that one the *warrior*.

'Just five,' I told him. 'When I fought Circe, I briefly brought others into being but I inhabited them briefly and had varying degrees of control over them. Since then there's just been the one warrior addition that you know about already.'

He nodded. 'Perhaps you should strive to double that number. But I won't presume to advise you concerning what form they should take. However, there is one thing that I must stress: as a tulpar, you have to be able to defend yourself against sometimes very formidable foes – something you found to your cost.'

'Foes such as Circe,' I added.

Hrothgar nodded. 'Yes, I speak of the goddess Circe, of course, and although that danger is now past there will be others. Tulpars such as we attract the attention of powerful adversaries. Perhaps it is jealousy or maybe even outrage that we are so skilled in such creative processes? Who knows, but Circe was not the first powerful being with whom I have less than cordial dealings. The majority of your tulpas should be able to defend themselves. You need to develop other tulpas that can fight aggressively like your new warrior body. Do I make myself clear?'

'Very clear,' I said. 'I thought being a spook was dangerous but this sounds even worse!'

'It can be,' said Hrothgar, 'but need not always be so. I do not actively seek danger like a spook. I do not ply a trade that brings me into frequent contact with the dark. I think of myself more as a scholar, a seeker after truth and knowledge, the getting of which is its own reward.'

I nodded but didn't reply immediately. I too was filled with curiosity and would be happy to pursue knowledge for its own sake, like a scholar at a university. However, I was also interested in what spooks such as Tom Ward did. They actively fought the dark and tried to make the County safe. I'd been a spook's apprentice for a while and that might well be the rough direction that the course of my own life might eventually follow. My conscience told me that I should use such skills that I acquired for the good of all.

Hrothgar came to his feet. 'I will leave you now, Wulf and Tilda, and return to my own demanding tasks. Work here whenever you like, read, think and dream. But first get some sleep – you must be tired after your journey. Tomorrow, when you are ready, go to the Temple and begin your first act of creation.'

He was referring to the Temple of Dreams, the room used for the creation of the type of tulpas called 'wraiths'. All bound tulpas were wraiths, but there was another room where materials such as dust, bones and blood were used to create the tulpas called 'gristles'. Those were used as servants by Hrothgar and I had already decided that I would never create a gristle.

That type of tulpa had no idea what it was. Were it ever to learn the truth about itself, the creature would instantly start to disintegrate and cease to exist – but not before first experiencing the terrible anguish of understanding exactly what it was. I was determined never to create such a gristle – capable of being tormented in that way.

That was what I truly believed at the time.

How wrong I was.

After a good sleep, we ate again with Hrothgar in the dining room. We called it breakfast but, here in this underworld, there was no distinction between day and night. The sky was always red, the colour of arterial blood.

Hrothgar was preoccupied, deep in thought, and we all concentrated on eating and spoke little. However, there was one important thing that I did need to ask of him.

'Once, the very first time I stayed with you, I had a shock when I left. Fourteen years had passed in the human world! Could I please ask you to use your magic again as on our previous visit to make sure that time passes at the same rate here as it does on the outside?'

Tilda had been a baby when I first entered this place and began my training. After what seemed just a few weeks, I'd returned to Chipenden to discover that she was a fourteen-year-old girl. I didn't want something like that happening again. On our last visit together, it had not been a problem.

'Fear not, Wulf. I will make sure that is the case. The first time I was under the control of Circe and it was that evil goddess who made me cause that large discrepancy in time. It will not happen again. On your last visit I controlled time for you. You need not worry because I will continue to do so. When one hour passes within this underworld, the same exact hour of time will also pass outside.'

Tilda was also capable of balancing time in the same way, but he was the master here and I had felt it right to ask that he be the one to do it now. I was happy with his reassurances.

With those words, Hrothgar left us to finish our breakfast and went off to work on his important tasks. I wondered what they could be but had decided not to ask him about it. It was his business, not mine, and if he ever wanted me to know what it was he would tell me.

We went straight to the library and directly to the desk where writing materials were kept. I brought to the table a pen, a bottle of ink and a couple of sheets of paper. Then I sat down and started to consider the possible forms of new bound tulpas that I could create, jotting each one down.

While I worked, Tilda consulted other books in the library – those which dealt with topics other than those that just concerned a tulpar. She was busy learning and trying to widen and strengthen her own magical abilities.

I didn't feel particularly inspired but just noted down each idea that drifted into my head. There weren't many of them.

A large dog that can hunt and fight.
Something that can live underground – maybe
  burrow?
A creature that can live in water without breathing
  air.

I stared at the paper but nothing more would come into my head. Maybe I shouldn't force it? I could make a start with one of the ideas I already had and wait for further inspiration.

No sooner had I decided that than I did get a flash of an idea that I knew was right. I already had a sky wolf but, rather than a large dog, why not create a true wolf tulpa! It would be a very powerful wolf capable of moving at speed and seeing off any other four-legged adversary – or even a two-legged human if necessary. To have such a body would be very useful.

But there were no longer any wolves in the County – or at least I didn't think so. Such a creature would draw attention to itself and it certainly couldn't enter a town without causing alarm. So why not create a wolf and a dog as well? The latter could be a small mongrel that could wander anywhere at will, even into a bustling market, and not be remarked upon, being taken for a stray. After all, despite Hrothgar's advice, not each one of my bound tulpas needed to be able to fight. Before facing danger, it was useful to be able to see the lie of the land and do so unnoticed by potential enemies.

That decision made, I came to my feet and suggested we go for a walk.

'Where to?' asked Tilda.

I shrugged, but before we left the library I was tempted to take a look at something close by. After once showing it to Tilda, it was a temptation I'd resisted many times but now my curiosity finally got the better of me.

'Let's take another look at that mysterious door,' I suggested.

There was a locked door which was out of sight round the corner. I'd once tried and failed to open it. I led us over to a library door which was perfectly ordinary and wasn't locked. I opened it and we entered a long narrow passageway, which had no windows and was furnished with small torches in brackets attached to the walls. As I walked forward, our presence automatically activated Hrothgar's magic and they flared with bright yellow light and lit the corridor.

The mysterious locked door, painted black, was the usual shape, being very high and designed to accommodate Hrothgar. It was right at the end of the corridor, and had no lock – not even a handle to grasp. It was made out of sturdy wood reinforced with metal plates, so there was no hope of breaking it using physical force.

I slowly walked towards it and on impulse became Saint Quentin, then stretched out my long bony arm and placed my palm against the door. Some inner mechanism clicked and whirred within it, as it had the previous time that I'd tried and failed to open it. That had been the only occasion when Saint Quentin had ever failed to open a locked door.

Tilda watched as I persisted for a minute at the most. I hadn't expected to be successful but a shiver of fear ran down my spine, and what made me cease was a sudden hunch that something dangerous might be hidden behind that door. Tilda had once tried and failed to open it too and she'd thought that there was something mysterious within.

Underworlds could be a bridge between the human world and Hell. There was a real danger that this was a doorway to the dark. If so, why would Hrothgar have such a door in his house? It was true that he had once been controlled by the dark goddess Circe. Could that be the reason?

As I became Wulf again, I thought of something else – another scary thought.

'Until now I've assumed that the door is locked in order to stop anyone in the house from opening it,' I said to Tilda. 'But I realize that's absurd. Apart from our visits, the only person in the house with access to this door is Hrothgar himself. So the most likely reason for the powerful locking mechanism is to stop something getting out and into this house.'

'There you are, Wulf, cheerful as usual and always looking for trouble!' mocked Tilda. 'It might just be to make sure that guests like us don't go nosing about where they're not invited! Hrothgar is entitled to a little privacy, don't you think?'

'I suppose you're right, Tilda. It's just that it is an incredibly powerful lock. Even as Saint Quentin, I can't get past it!'

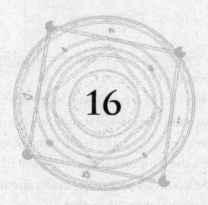

16

PIDDLE

Five days passed quickly and I worked really hard at developing my skills, often spending time in the Temple while Tilda studied in the library.

I sat at the table, rested my chin on my hands, closed my eyes and conjured a memory. At the abbey, the monks who worked in the kitchen were always having to drive away stray dogs made sly and brave by their hunger.

There was one particular dog that exceeded them all, a small grey-coated mongrel. It was a thin, wiry creature that I remembered well because it had a tail that reminded me of one more usually found on a rat. It also had something of the crafty bravery of such creatures.

There was another unusual thing about that little dog. It never barked. It just gave the occasional grunt and also had a reputation of piddling in corners, an unhygienic habit that particularly annoyed the monks.

I once saw it run at a monk and seize a hunk of bread right out of his hand. He chased it and the little dog dropped the bread. Then, before he could react, it ran through his legs, leaped up onto the table and seized the meat from his plate. Then it escaped with its prize. The crafty animal had used the bread to get what it *really* wanted.

I concentrated and tried to create that mongrel, working hard to see it clearly in my imagination. I was getting better at this. It had been easier to create the sky wolf than Raphael, the first of my bound tulpas. Practice was developing my skills and it wasn't long before I could see the dog in my mind's eye, exactly as I remembered, right down to the thin grey rat tail.

I slowly counted down from five to zero, a trick that Hrothgar had taught me in order to achieve focus. When I reached zero, I breathed out with force and opened my eyes.

I heard a noise – a faint panting – and the small dog was there at my feet, staring up at me with its tongue lolling from its mouth.

It only persisted for a couple of seconds before fading away. But I had brought my new wraith into the world. I was slightly disappointed that I had not looked out through its eyes – an indication that I had achieved a tulpa that was bound and therefore one sharing a splinter of my soul and a part of me. But there was still time for that.

It was a good beginning.

Later, at supper, despite my concern that he might be annoyed at my meddling in what he probably considered to be his own private business, I asked Hrothgar about the black door.

'There's a locked door at the end of the corridor that leads from the library. What's beyond it?' I asked.

I saw Tilda dart me a look of annoyance. I hadn't warned her that I was going to question Hrothgar about the door. I know she would have liked me to mention it to her first. That's why I hadn't done so. I thought she might have tried to talk me out of it.

Hrothgar chewed very slowly and seemed to ignore my question. When he finally looked at me directly, his expression was grim and far from friendly. 'You would be far better employed concentrating on the tasks that we agreed upon, rather than poking your nose into something which does not concern you!' he snapped.

Although it was his right to refuse to answer my question, the manner in which he did so annoyed me. I felt angry at being talked to in that way, especially in front of Tilda, and I challenged him with my reply.

'When you feigned death and left all your property to me, I explored it thoroughly and, on finding the door, tried to open it. After all, at the time I thought it belonged to me. I have been intrigued ever since.'

That answer reminded him of how he had deceived me and, although under duress, had behaved in a way that could have led to the death of Tilda at the hands of the evil goddess Circe.

'It was certainly excusable then,' replied Hrothgar, his tone becoming milder, 'but the situation has changed. You have come here of your own free will in response to my open invitation in order to continue your training. I am happy to facilitate that but you are both guests in my house and I expect you to abide by my rules. Stay away from that door, Wulf. And I say the same to you, Tilda. I forbid you to approach it!'

I nodded. 'We will do as you ask. As you say, it is your house and that door is your business so it is not for me to pry. But I'm naturally curious and a mystery like that nags at me, making it difficult to put it from my mind.'

Hrothgar sighed, pushed his plate away and came to his feet. 'For your sake as well as mine, Wulf, please curb your curiosity. Were you to open that door we should all regret it. There are some things it is better not to know – things that we should thrust from our minds forever.'

*

The following morning, after breakfast, I went straight to the Temple of Dreams and continued working on the dog tulpa.

It proved even easier than the previous day. Once more I opened my eyes to find the tulpa staring up at me, its thin tail wagging. A moment later I was filled with a sense of achievement as I found myself looking out through the eyes of the dog. I was staring up at an empty chair!

The human tulpa, shaped like the flesh and blood human that I had once been, had vanished. I'd done it with ease! I had already created a new bound tulpa. I opened my mouth and tried to bark. All that came out was a grunt. That was exactly what I'd intended.

I named the tulpa Piddle!

I ran round the table three times full of exultation then came to a halt and began to explore my new senses. In the body of the sky wolf, I'd delighted in flight, and one of the first things I'd become aware of was enhanced vision. Not only could I focus my eyes to see small objects at a great distance, I could even see currents of air that appeared to me as different shades. I could see the warm brown thermals that could carry me aloft and that greatly advanced my flying skills.

Now inside the body of this small mongrel my eyesight hardly seemed better than that of a human but the big change was to my sense of smell. The remaining odour of my human tulpa wasn't very strong but I could detect smells of food from the kitchen and, more distantly, the scent of grass from the lawn and the foliage and from the trees that encircled the house and its garden.

Happy with that success I decided to try to create a bound wolf tulpa next.

That proved to be easier. Remembering my concern that the County no longer had wolves and that if spotted by humans it would draw unwelcome attention to itself, I made its fur as black as possible. That way, after dark, it could move through the countryside almost invisible.

I named it Black Fang.

Although our future meetings were still cordial, during the week that followed, I sensed a clear cooling of the warmth that Hrothgar had formerly shown towards me. I saw little of him, but when we were in sight of each other he was more likely to scowl rather than give me a friendly smile as he did formerly.

One morning, things came to a head when he walked into the library and, with just the briefest of nods, sat down in his huge leather armchair. Tilda and I nodded back, smiled and continued making notes. In addition to developing my new tulpas, I was still gathering information about my new craft. But, a little unnerved by the silence and the fact that he seemed to be watching me carefully, on impulse I asked another question.

'Martha, the tulpa who lives in the cottage and buys our groceries in the village – is she the same tulpa who served you before Circe imprisoned you?' I asked. 'Or is she just something similar, a copy that will pass in the outside world when she visits the village to buy provisions?'

When I had returned to the underworld for the first time, Mother Martha and his other tulpa servants had vanished, and the only tulpa left had been the abhuman who had shown me Hrothgar's grave, pretending that his master was dead. Later, the abhuman too had disappeared.

'It is the same Martha, the same tulpa. As you know, the way to end a gristle is simply to tell it its true nature but I did not do that. Whatever you were told then was communicated under duress. I was being controlled by Circe but I stored Martha, my cook and the abhuman in case I needed them again. And now enough of your questions! I came here to tell you that, for a while, this library is out of bounds to you both. You must not come here again until I give you permission. I have vital work to do here, tasks that must be done alone and beyond the eyes of others.'

'Of course,' I said, as we came to our feet. 'We'll go and work in our rooms.'

'I suggest that you first search these shelves and select any books that might prove useful in your studies. Take as many as you wish and store them in your rooms. I will not start until tomorrow so you have until supper.'

We both thanked him politely and he came to his feet and prepared to leave. Then he paused. 'Oh! And just one more thing. The staff that belongs to your father – take that with you also, Tilda, and keep it in your room.'

When Hrothgar had left, I thought carefully about what he'd said and things started to come together in my mind. So I explained my suspicions to Tilda.

'Why does he want to perform some important task *here* in the library? I can understand that he might wish to be away from our prying eyes but wouldn't he be better off working in the Temple of Dreams or the Gristle Room? But I can think of one very good reason why this might suit his purposes better, Tilda. This library gives access to the locked door. It's the only way to reach it. So, does his task have something to do with what's beyond it?'

'I think you could well be right, Wulf,' Tilda said. 'But, as he keeps telling us, it's none of our business.'

'But why has he become so unfriendly?' I asked. 'He's changing and I don't like it.'

'Maybe what he's trying to do is difficult and dangerous and he's under a big strain,' Tilda said. 'That could be making him the way he is. We should just let him get on with it. I'm sure he knows what he's doing and, once he's accomplished it, he'll probably go back to being his usual friendly and helpful self.'

I shrugged. I wasn't sure that Tilda was right. I still had my doubts and fears but for now I stopped talking about them. Time would tell.

After browsing the shelves, we collected about three dozen books. Some were quite large and heavy and it took us several trips before they were all neatly stacked on the tables in our rooms. Lastly, I carried the Spook's staff away and offered it to Tilda to keep safe. She certainly wanted her father's staff but, being a witch, although able to carry it, she did not like the touch of rowan wood. So, at her suggestion, I carried it into her room for her and left it leaning against the wall.

That was another puzzle. What did it matter whether the staff was in the library or not? It had been there for a very long time and took up so little room.

If it bothered him so much, why hadn't Hrothgar moved it himself?

Could it be, I wondered, suspicions bubbling up into my mind again, that he *could* not touch it, like the darkest and most evil witches? In that case he really had changed for the worse. We were both tulpars, with the same gifts, but I had no difficulty at all in touching rowan wood.

Then I had another thought. He had said that he had stored his tulpas. Could he have kept them somewhere beyond that locked door? If so, what other things were stored behind it?

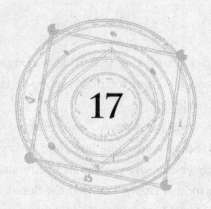

17

WOLF GRISTLES

Two nights later, I was awoken by a terrible screaming from somewhere in the house. For one moment I thought it was Tilda, but she was already outside my door when I emerged still tugging on my boots.

'The screams are coming from the library!' she cried.

We ran there immediately but it was deserted. By now the screams had stopped. Everything was silent, the tables were clear of books and there was no evidence at all that anyone had been there recently. I had expected that Hrothgar would have been drawn there by those terrible sounds. But who could have gained access to the house? Not only would an intruder need to find a way into this underworld but they would then have to contend with the fearsome guardians that lurked within the trees.

That left only one logical possibility.

It was Hrothgar who'd been screaming.

Our eyes met and Tilda and I both realized at the same moment where the screams had been coming from.

We opened the other door and walked into the passageway. The torches ignited one by one as we walked its length to reach the locked door. As we stared at it another shrill scream pierced the silence.

That sound of torment came from behind that mysterious black door.

I moved close to it. 'Hrothgar! Hrothgar! Is that you?' I shouted.

In response there was a terrible groaning from behind the door. 'Yes, Wulf! Listen to me carefully. There is not much time!'

'Open the door! Let us help!' I shouted.

'No!' said Hrothgar, giving another groan of pain. 'I am dying. Soon after I am dead, dangerous entities may attempt to get through the door and out into the world. You must not open the door for anything. I will no longer be able to help, so you must guard the door at all times.'

'Who are they?' I asked.

At first he did not reply, just screamed again. Then he began to give me further instructions but I had to put my ear against the door because his voice was becoming fainter.

'After I am gone all my tulpas will cease to be. Guarding the door and the underworld will become *your* responsibility.

You must create your own tulpas to prevent anything coming through the door. You must create gristles! They *must* be gristles! Do you understand? Bound wraiths are no good because you cannot spend all your time in their bodies, on guard. You must make gristles independent of yourself to guard the door. You will need gristles to guard the underworld too. You must defend the house against the dangers from without as well as dangers from within . . .'

'Let us in, Hrothgar!' I called through the door. 'We can save you!'

'Nobody can help me now. Think of yourselves. Think of the safety of the world too. Please! Please do as I say . . .'

His voice was hardly more than a whisper.

'I am going,' he said. 'Soon nothing of me will remain . . .'

When I spoke his name again, he did not reply.

It was an hour or so before we left the door. It seemed callous to just walk away and leave him to his fate. But it was Tilda who took my hand and tugged me away.

'There's nothing that we can do for him, Wulf,' she said. 'I think he's gone and now you should do what he says.'

She was right. I believed that Hrothgar was already dead or, if not, he had been dragged away to a place where he would be slain. A terrible danger must lurk behind that door.

We went to the kitchen and Tilda told me to sit down while she made us both a hot drink. We sat at the table but didn't speak for a while, both lost in our thoughts about what had happened.

'If Hrothgar is dead, or taken to the dark, then all the gristles will be dead now without him to animate them – the cook, Martha at the cottage and the big beasts in the trees that guard the inside of the gate,' Tilda said. 'If someone or something breaks through into the underworld there'll be nothing to stop them. We need to do something about that but the first and most important need is to guard that door.'

Whatever had killed Hrothgar would probably want to kill me, I realized fearfully. I had never felt really close to him so I didn't feel the same degree of sadness that perhaps I should. But I had respected him and I did feel a strong sense of loss. He had done his best to train me. He had also once saved my life when one of my own tulpas was trying to destroy me.

'Can you make a gristle?' Tilda interrupted my thoughts.

'Well, we've read Hrothgar's books about that. We both know *how* to do it but I never intended to make one.'

'Well, if you make a gristle in the form of an animal, it won't be as bad as making something with a human mind. Then it will never know the truth about itself. So you won't need to worry your conscience about that.'

I nodded. 'Will you help me, Tilda?'

'Of course I will. I don't think there is a moment to waste. We should start right now.'

Firstly, Tilda helped me to prepare the Gristle Room. We carefully swept the flags and cleared a space for us to work. Then together we carried sacks of material from the store sheds, which were adjacent to the rear of the house, across to the Gristle Room. Some sacks contained bone fragments and dust, others a mixture of soft clay and soggy leaves. I started by shaping a heap of material on the flags that very crudely resembled the shape of the gristle that I was going to try and create. I roughed out the form of a huge wolf lying on its side.

I used a lot of material. I wanted the tulpa to be large and formidable.

Next, while Tilda kept away to the far side of the room, I began to concentrate, trying very hard to see in my mind's eye a very clear image of the tulpa that I was about to create. It was almost exactly the same process as when creating a wraith. What differed was the need to hold the image of the shaped materials in my mind too and bring it into the other image to add substance to it. That required even more concentration than usual.

I closed my eyes and brought all the power of my imagination to bear upon the task. But I tried three times to make the gristle and failed each time. I used all the techniques that Hrothgar had taught me, including counting down to zero – the moment of maximum effort. But, each time when I opened my eyes, I was faced with the same pile of inert materials.

I knew from experience that it could sometimes take long hours, days even, to create a tulpa. What was needed was an accumulation of effort. Sometimes it was relatively easy – on other occasions much harder. It was important to carry on trying.

'You look tired,' said Tilda. 'Perhaps you should get some sleep and try again when you're refreshed?'

'There's great danger behind that door, Tilda. We can't afford to sleep until some level of protection has been achieved.'

'In that case, there's something else that might help. Remember what we read in the books when we first found out how to make a gristle tulpa? Blood helps, doesn't it?'

I nodded. 'Yes, but it's not vital. Somehow I don't like the idea of using blood . . .'

'It's no worse than using fragments of bone,' she said. 'And it might just help.'

'I think that Hrothgar used animal blood. But we don't have any animals.'

'Why don't we use human blood?' Tilda suggested. 'From what I remember reading about the process, it doesn't take a lot – a few drops for each tulpa – that's all you'd need.'

I still didn't like the idea. It reminded me too much of the way that some witches fed their own blood to their familiars but I could see no immediate alternative. 'Then I'll use some of my blood,' I conceded.

'No!' Tilda said, stepping closer to me. 'We should use *my* blood.'

'No!' I protested. 'I can't let you do that.'

'Think about it, Wulf. My blood should be more effective than yours. After all, I have the blood of powerful witches in my veins – not to mention the lamia blood that my father inherited from his mam and he must have passed on to me. My blood is special. That's why Circe wanted it so much! It's probably the best blood in the whole world for making a gristle!'

That was true enough. Using Tilda's blood, Circe had hoped to be able to gain enough power to walk the earth permanently during the hours of daylight – something that the Old Gods could not do.

It was hard to argue against that. 'We'll try it,' I told Tilda.

She grinned and left the room, returning about five minutes later holding a small narrow bottle. In the bottom of it there was about half an inch of her blood. As she held it up before me, I noticed the small bandage twisted round the middle finger of her left hand. Then Tilda walked across to the heap of clay, soggy leaves, pieces of bone and dust that I had shaped upon the flags. She held the bottle over it and tipped a few drops onto it.

'Now try again,' she said.

I did.

It still didn't work.

I kept trying . . . and on the fifth attempt I heard a growl. I opened my eyes to see a big scary wolf staring straight into my eyes, its jaws open like it was ready to pounce and eat me.

It wasn't quite the same as Black Fang – the wraith I had created – nor exactly the picture that I'd held in my mind's eye, but it was close enough. Perhaps the use of Tilda's blood had changed the tulpa slightly? This wolf was grey rather than black, and a somewhat sleeker animal, not quite so burly but probably better suited to speed.

Despite its fearsome appearance, it didn't attack either of us. It just lost interest in me and walked over to Tilda. It licked her hands and then she began to pat it.

'This is a very large wolf,' Tilda said. 'My father said that Bill Arkwright used to have two creatures similar to this but they were part wolf, part dog. They were called Tooth and Claw.'

'Those are good names!' I said. 'So we'll call this one *Tooth* and the next one *Claw*. I heard somewhere that Bill had two more dogs after that but I can't remember their names.'

'Looks like I've got a better memory than you!' Tilda said triumphantly. 'They were called Blood and Bone and that's another two more names! So now we've got four and just need another two.'

I carried on until, over an hour later, I had created a second gristle which we named Claw.

At first, I had wondered how I'd get the gristles to do what I wanted. Would I have to train the grey wolves in the same way that you trained a dog to be obedient? But it quickly became apparent that wouldn't be necessary. I only had to wish for them to behave as I wanted and they did exactly that. I could almost feel their minds rubbing against mine like a hint of warm fur. I couldn't inhabit their bodies as I could with the sky wolf, Raphael and the other bound wraiths, but there was a very strong link between me and my creations and, sometimes, they felt almost like extensions of myself.

I positioned Tooth to guard the door and left the house taking Claw with us down the steps and into the trees. There we found the remains of Hrothgar's guardian gristles that had died and disintegrated. There were big ugly mounds of clay, leaves and small pieces of bone. I'd never seen one of those guardian creatures close up, just heard them snuffling, roaring and growling, hidden by the trees, but they must have been as huge and fearsome as they sounded.

It was best not to feed the gristles yet. According to Hrothgar's books, this type of gristle designed to fight was always hungry which made it more dangerous. The truth was that they did not require any food to maintain their form. It was an incentive, not a need.

Enemies were food.

'Stay!' I told Claw and he settled down on his haunches and I left him there to guard the entrance to the underworld.

Tilda gave the tulpa a final pat before we walked away. After that, we slept. I was exhausted.

The next morning, we returned to the Gristle Room and, with the help of more drops of Tilda's blood, I created an additional four creatures. Now we had six grey wolves so three were set to guard the door; the three others guarded the gate.

We'd named the fifth and sixth tulpas Hide and Hair.

'What now?' I asked Tilda. The death of Hrothgar and the danger that still waited behind the locked door had unsettled me. It would be difficult to just go back to the routine of my studies.

'It's your decision,' said Tilda. 'You're the tulpar and now I suppose this house and underworld belongs to you.'

I supposed that was true. After all, when he'd faked his death previously, Hrothgar had left the house to me. Now that he was truly dead, I assumed that the same applied. I certainly didn't expect a lawyer to visit anytime soon to argue about it.

'I'm still thinking things through,' I told Tilda. 'There are a lot of mysteries here, questions that need to be answered. We need to do something but I'm not sure what. So, while we're making up our minds about what to do, I suppose I could try and continue my training using the library.'

She nodded. 'While you're occupied with that, I'll do some research myself. Surely, somewhere in one of those books, there must be something about that door. How did it come to be? Was it built with the house? Or did it already exist, and the house was built round it so as to contain the danger? There's got to be something about it *somewhere* in this house – either in one of the books from the library or recorded elsewhere in Hrothgar's own hand.'

'And what were the special tasks that Hrothgar was attempting to complete?' I added. 'Was the danger increasing and did he attempt to halt the threat in some way? But, if so, why did he open the door and go inside?'

'Or did something escape and drag him in there, closing the door behind it?' asked Tilda.

I hoped that the three grey wolf tulpas would be enough to keep the door secure. At least they would give us a warning if anything started to happen there . . .

Suddenly I remembered something and became alarmed. 'Tilda! What about time outside, now that Hrothgar's dead?'

'Somebody with a good memory has to think about what's important,' she said with a smile. 'I remembered that before you began working on the tulpas. I've used my magic to take care of it.'

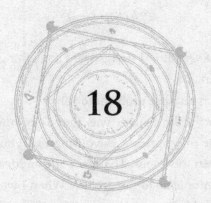

18

A SNIFFING AT THE DOOR

We quickly got back into a routine again. It was mostly study, but my favourite diversion was to take the wolves out through the gate each day into the outer world of the cloudy County. Tilda and I took turns, each of us taking three.

The first time I did that, I checked the cottage that was close to the two trees that marked the gateway to the underworld. As I expected, inside I found a heap of clothing filled with dust, clay and tiny fragments of bone.

It was all that was left of Martha.

Her remains reminded me that she was the one who went down into the village to buy provisions. Within a week or so at the most we would run out of food, but the village must be avoided because it drew attention to us. Once, a few years earlier, after displaying her magical powers, Tilda had been reported to a Quisitor. I didn't want something like that to happen again.

So that was another problem to solve.

My run with the wolves was fun. They hunted rabbits and ate their prey quickly, devouring everything – blood, flesh and even the bones. That gave me an idea which was easy to communicate to the gristles. When I went back into the underworld, I was carrying three extra dead rabbits that the wolves had hunted for me.

We couldn't live on rabbits alone but it did help our situation.

Once back at the house, I set my three grey wolves to guard the locked door. Now it was Tilda's turn to take the other three for a run.

So it went on, two or three days passing quickly. Perhaps I should have realized the danger. I should have guessed what Tilda intended to do but I was too busy planning more tulpas. I was thinking about it very carefully, drawing up a long list from which I would make my final selections. This time these would be wraiths, bodies that I could use. Despite my strong liking for the grey wolves, I certainly had no desire to create any more gristles.

I awoke one morning expecting to join Tilda for breakfast. I searched almost everywhere, calling her name over and over again but she had vanished from the house.

My heart sank as I knew immediately where she must be.

I could hear the wolves whining as soon as I entered the library. I went through into the passageway and approached the locked door. The three creatures were on their bellies with their snouts almost touching it.

I went onto my knees, pushing them aside and resting my forehead against the door.

'Tilda! Tilda!' I called.

'Oh, Wulf! I'm so sorry!' Tilda replied from behind the door. 'I'm so sorry. I was foolish to do this. Now I can't get out. I'm trapped.'

I was more than a little angry with her for not telling me what she'd been up to. But that was nothing compared to my fear for Tilda. I remembered how Hrothgar's voice had gradually got weaker and weaker as he told us that something was killing him.

'How did you get inside, Tilda?' I asked, trying to keep my voice calm.

'I used my magic. I've been working on a spell for days and I finally got it right. But as soon as I got inside, this stupid door slammed shut behind me and I was trapped.'

'Can't you use the same spell to open it again and get out?' I asked.

'It doesn't work, Wulf. I tried and tried all night, but the door remained shut. Then I attempted something else and finally learned the awful truth. My magic doesn't work inside here!'

I went cold at the thought. If the thing that had been killing Hrothgar came back, Tilda would have no defence against it.

'What can you see inside there?' I asked.

'It's just a narrow tunnel – not more than about twelve feet or so long and less than three feet wide but at least eleven feet high. That must be to accommodate Hrothgar. This passageway was made for him to use. There are torches on the walls just like the ones where you are. And there's another door at the far end.'

'What kind of door?' I asked.

'It looks exactly the same as this one and it's locked too. As my magic doesn't work in here, I can't open it . . .'

'Don't even try!' I said, raising my voice without meaning to. Hrothgar had warned of the danger of something getting out. Whatever terrible entity that was would be lurking somewhere behind that second door.

'There's something else,' said Tilda. 'There's a patch of dried blood on the floor and a trail of it leading to the other door.'

Tilda said nothing more and I couldn't think of anything to say to reassure her. Something had dragged Hrothgar through the doorway. We sat there in silence but for the low whining of the grey wolves who were clearly unhappy at being deprived of contact with Tilda. I knew she had to be afraid. I would have been terrified.

Although I had little hope of success, I had to try something so I took on the shape of Saint Quentin and placed my bony hand against the door. Once more there was the sound of some hidden mechanism responding, but then it fell silent and the door didn't open.

The hours that followed were among the worst that I'd ever experienced. I had little comfort to offer Tilda and she didn't have much to say either. I stayed by the door. I was hungry, but if Tilda couldn't eat then neither would I.

At one point, Tilda was silent for so long that I thought she might have fallen asleep. I wasn't sure whether to speak or remain silent. She was better off asleep and away from the situation so I didn't want to wake her. And yet, if she was simply sitting there awake and terrified it was better for me to say something. Suddenly, while I was still struggling to make up my mind, Tilda asked me a question.

'Are the wolves sniffing at the door?'

'No. They are lying at my side. Two have their eyes closed and Blood is staring at the door. Why?'

'It's just that I can hear a sniffing sound. Wait a moment . . .'

After a few seconds' silence she spoke again but Tilda's voice was much lower. It was hard to hear what she said. I shouted for her to repeat it and then she must have moved closer to the far door. But I had heard what she said first time and it sent chills of fear for Tilda up my spine.

'The sound's coming from the other door, Wulf. Something's sniffing at it – some kind of creature.'

'Keep perfectly still,' I told her. 'Don't speak for a while. It might just go away.'

As the new silence lengthened, I tried to tell myself that she was in no real danger. After all, the entity that had fed upon Hrothgar, then dragged him away, had been inside the passageway with him. Or at least it had seemed that way, although he'd not actually said that. But it had to be next to him or how else could it have been eating him?

Hopefully, this was something else, something different, and couldn't get inside.

It must have been at least fifteen minutes before Tilda spoke again. I was relieved at hearing her voice and what she said eased my fears a little.

'I think it's gone,' she said.

'It couldn't get in,' I said. 'Maybe you're safer than we think. It could be that the thing that killed Hrothgar only preys upon tulpars? It may not be a danger to you.'

'Maybe,' she replied, not sounding convinced. 'But I can't survive here for very long, can I? I could go without food for a long time – days and days, maybe even weeks – but not without water. My throat is dry already. Without water I could be dead inside three days.'

'I'll try again, using Saint Quentin!' I said, trying to give her hope.

'No,' Tilda said. 'You've done your best and that doesn't work. There's only one person that I know who might be able to free me. You need to bring my mother to this door – Alice might be able to do it.'

'It would mean leaving you alone here, Tilda . . .'

'You wouldn't be leaving me alone for long. If I'm right, it might just seem like a few minutes to me. That's the good news. The bad news is that a lot of time might have passed outside the underworld.'

My heart sank as I realized what Tilda meant. Not only did her magic fail to work behind the door, spells that she'd used outside might have failed by now. In that case the underworld's passage of time would be unstable. It might have continued in the same way but, alternatively, it might have reverted to the way it had once been or become even more extreme. Years might be speeding by outside. In that case, the sooner I went for help, the better.

'I'll go for help now, Tilda. If you're right it will seem just like minutes to you.'

'Take care, Wulf,' she called.

I was already racing for the front door of the house. Once outside and well clear of it, I changed one tulpa body for another. Within seconds I had become the sky wolf. I could vary this tulpa's size so I made it as large as I could. That meant I would be able to fly faster. That would also limit my endurance but, as the crow flies, Chipenden was well within range.

I beat my huge black wings and soared aloft, heading towards the invisible gate that lay between the two tall sycamores.

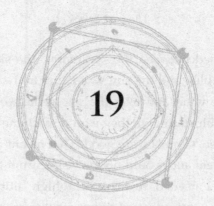

19

MIRROR WRITING

I hoped that not too much time had passed but my mind was churning with terrible possibilities. What if the underworld had compensated for having been forced, for so long, to maintain the same speed of time as on the outside?

What if minutes within now meant that many years had already passed outside the underworld?

In that case Alice and Tom might no longer be alive and I would get no help for Tilda. But the opposite also brought a terrible danger.

If time was still passing at the same rate both within and outside the underworld, then every second that I was away increased the threat she faced. At any moment, some creature might find its way into the passageway and kill her. Even if that didn't happen, I would have to find Alice and bring her back here before Tilda died of thirst.

As I passed between the sycamores, the sky changed from red to blue and the sun was rising in the east. There was a fierce wind and over the sea to the west a line of clouds was blustering in; they would reach me within five minutes or so. Clouds were good. That meant that I could fly above them and would not be visible from the ground. Otherwise, I needed to achieve a high altitude which would deplete my energy. I didn't want to scare too many people. Neither did I want to draw undue attention to myself.

Who knew what enemies were lurking out there?

Firstly, I needed to take a look at the village. It looked like late autumn to me – the trees and hedgerows were denuded and fallen leaves littered the grass. But which autumn? Which year? How much time had elapsed?

As I flew over the village at a higher altitude, my heart sank. It was much larger than previously, with almost twice as many houses and a new road leading into it from the east. At the usual rate that County villages grew that would have taken years – but how many?

I gained more altitude and flew directly towards Chipenden just as fast as I could, driven by the urgency of the threat to Tilda. It had been a while since I'd last used the sky wolf tulpa and, despite my anxieties, I delighted in the experience. To fly was exhilarating. My vision was much sharper than that possible for human eyes and I could see the ground below in great detail: farmers out in their fields, travellers on the roads between the villages and towns. There seemed to be lots of small groups heading southwest and they were mostly women.

As I moved further inland, high clouds obscured the sun and below me were other faster ones that hid the ground from my gaze. As soon as I approached the edge of the Bowland Fells, their summits like islands above a grey sea, it began to rain hard. That torrential downpour lasted until I was soaring somewhere above Chipenden village, but as I descended towards the Spook's house, the clouds broke and the sun began to shine brightly.

I landed in a field close to the withy trees crossroads and took on the first of my two human shapes, the one that Tilda preferred, that of the boy I had been when we had first spent time together in Hrothgar's house. I had aged that tulpa a couple of years but, apart from that and being a couple of inches taller, it was essentially the same figure.

I walked past the bell and saw that it was in good order, the rope hanging low so that anyone who called on spook's business could ring the bell to call Tom. As I entered the garden, I heard the blind boggart growl just once and then remain silent. It knew me of old and was aware that I had Tom's permission to be there.

If Tom was away on a job, at least Alice should be at home and she was the one that I had come to see and take back with me. I noted that the lawn area had been scythed recently and the house looked well maintained, so that was reassuring. But when I knocked at the door there was no response.

It would have taken me just moments to become Saint Quentin and open that door, but it was Tom and Alice's house and that would be rude. That wouldn't help me anyway. But where had they gone?

It was then that a shimmer of light caught my eye. It was on the path at the point where it curved round the house. There was a small puddle of rainwater but it was shining as if it was reflecting sunlight. But that wasn't possible because it was in the shade.

I walked close and immediately I saw the words. It was a message. Magic had been used here. Who else could it be from but Alice? But the message was in some strange language . . .

Wulf

Tom and I are in grave danger. We are the captives of a large gathering of covens who plan to raise the Fiend this very night. We are in Churchtown, which is on the southern bank of the Ribble estuary.

Alice

Then I realized that I was being stupid. Alice had once given me a mirror and told me to use it if I needed help.

Some witches used mirror writing to communicate, making it appear to be written backwards to the one who received it. My name was easy to read – it was meant for me and signed by Alice at the bottom.

It didn't take me long to make sense of the rest. Tom and Alice had been captured by witches who were trying to raise the Fiend. That puzzled me as I thought the Fiend had been destroyed many years earlier. Tilda had told me that Tom had played a big part in that. I also noted that Alice didn't actually ask directly for help. No doubt she was too proud after all the quarrels.

But even if I hadn't needed Alice to save Tilda, I would still have gone to her aid. Despite all that had happened, I till liked Alice. And as she was Tilda's mother I considered her to be part of my family too.

I'd never been to Churchtown, where they were being held captive, but it was on the southern bank of the Ribble estuary and shouldn't be too hard to find. So I left the garden quickly and, once clear of the trees, I became the sky wolf and took to the sky heading south. This time I made myself smaller to conserve energy.

It wasn't even noon, so I had time to reach Churchtown long before nightfall. But then my blood ran cold. How old was the message? In some way the spell had been triggered by my presence, but how long had it been waiting?

Grave danger? Tom and Alice might already be dead.

For all I knew the message might be many years old. I tried not to think about that possibility and flew on, passing high over Priestown and then following the southern bank of the Ribble towards the estuary. Soon I was flying over small groups of travellers heading in the same direction. Most of them seemed to be female. Were they witches? If so, that was good. It suggested that they were still gathering to summon the Fiend.

In that case, the ceremony hadn't taken place yet. There might still be time to save Tom and Alice.

As for finding Churchtown . . . well, if the name meant anything, that was easy. It was the only village with a large church and the only one with a steeple. One downward glance at the village green confirmed it. A huge bonfire had been built there and groups of witches were sitting on the grass surrounding it while more arrived by the minute.

I landed to the south well over two miles away. Then I took on another shape, this time one of my more recent wraith creations – I became Piddle, the small grey-coated mongrel dog with a tail that was more suited to a rat. Hopefully, it would be taken for a stray so the most danger I would attract was a kick.

It didn't take me long to reach Churchtown, and as I meandered across the green, wagging my tail and giving the occasional sniff at an interesting sweaty body, I did attract the odd lunge of a pointy shoe and once a poorly directed boot. There were men here too whose clothes held a delightful smell of rotten fish.

I was relieved that I was not too late. I noticed that many of the witches were sharing blood cakes that were traditionally consumed at each of the four dark sabbaths. It was late autumn so this must be the one called Halloween. This was the best time in the whole year for witches to summon the Fiend.

Where were the prisoners being held? If I could find them, I might have a chance of getting them out and away from here. I circled the bonfire, occasionally having a quick pee against that huge stack of wood and avoiding the occasional kick. This would be the Fiend's fiery throne. It deserved a good piddling.

Where was Alice? No sooner had the thought entered my head than I saw what I was looking for. A face appeared at a barred window of an inn on the edge of the green. Without doubt it was Alice. But I was shocked by her appearance – she looked so old. Many years had passed. Too many. But not too many to save Tilda. If Alice still had her magical power she might well be able to open that locked door.

But after sniffing around a little longer I decided against attempting a rescue now. The doors of the inn were guarded and there were witches all around it. So I would have to wait until the prisoners were brought out onto the green. That would also be dangerous and difficult. But it might just be possible despite so many of our enemies being present.

I would have to become the sky wolf again.

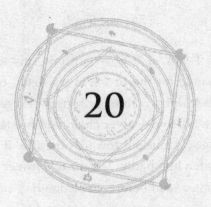

20

THE POINTY SPIRE

I suppose I had intended to attack the witches and scatter them. Once that was achieved, I would have returned to a human shape and led the prisoners to safety. There was no real detail to my plan. It was vague. I intended to improvise – make things up as I went along and hopefully be able to counter each danger as it arose.

I'd also hoped to accomplish that before the Fiend made his appearance. I'd no idea what he was capable of and it was safer not to risk confronting him. But that eventually became impossible because the prisoners were not led out onto the green until it was almost midnight.

I was very high above them. Even in daylight I would have been very difficult to see, just a tiny speck against the blue. But at night, although the sky was clear, I was as good as invisible.

Although I was at a great altitude, my acute vision made it possible for me to see every detail of what was happening below. I saw three prisoners dragged out. Alice was bound with Tom's silver chain and he staggered and limped as he was pushed towards the fire. It looked like they had beaten him badly. The third prisoner was a girl – one I had never seen before. Someone had scratched her face badly.

Then, before I could intervene, what I had feared happened. The Fiend suddenly appeared among the flames of the bonfire. He was big, taller even than Hrothgar. But whereas the tulpar had been skinny – so much so that, at first, I had privately called him 'the Thin Giant' – the Fiend was broad and muscular, his chest like a barrel, his whole body covered in thick black hair. His head was huge and to the sides of his forehead were enormous curved ram's horns.

I had expected to feel terror at the sight of one so evil and dangerous. As far as spooks were concerned, the Fiend was one among several Old Gods and had once been the most powerful. However, for me, one who had been trained for a while as a monk, he had a very special significance.

He was evil personified, the manifestation of Hell and a terrible threat to all that I believed in.

This was the enemy of the Church I had once served.

This was the Devil.

My feelings and response to his manifestation were a surprise to me. They erupted out of me like burning lava from a volcano. I was not afraid. No longer even nervous. Suddenly I was burning with anger and hatred. I wanted to hurt him very badly. I wanted to drive him from my sight and away from our world.

I realized that not all those feelings had my human self as their source. When I dwelt within its body, each wraith tulpa added something to me. It changed me at least temporarily. And the sky wolf loved combat. It was a taker of risks who would rather be destroyed than flee. And now it wanted the blood of the Fiend. It wanted to hurt him. It desired to rip and tear his flesh. It considered his very presence on earth an outrage and an affront.

Without fully realizing what I was doing, I began to fly away from the green, heading south and gaining even more altitude. I also increased my size to the maximum that I could.

That large size gave me strength but also had a distinct disadvantage. When small, I was capable of flying forever and a day because my expenditure of energy was small. Once grown to a size such as this, I could not maintain it for too long. And although capable of explosive bursts of speed and strength, I had not fed since leaving Tilda and the underworld. The flights to Chipenden and then Churchtown had depleted my strength severely.

I would get only one chance to carry out my attack. After that I would be exhausted until I fed again and my powers were renewed. If I failed, the three prisoners would suffer horrible deaths.

Sometimes, when in the body of the sky wolf, I stooped to my prey like a hawk, folding my wings and plummeting from the sky like a falling stone. This time, as I turned and flew back towards the bonfire, I was descending rapidly at about thirty degrees to the ground, beating my wings as fast as I could to gain maximum speed.

There was a line of trees right on the edge of the green and I wished that they were about eight feet lower. I could estimate the path of my flight and those treetops spoiled the perfect line of my attack. I needed to pass over them as low as possible.

Now, as I came in fast and low, barely clearing their tops, the wind created by my approach made the tips of their lower branches bend and kiss the grass.

My jaws were open wide, fangs at the ready, my talons outstretched in eagerness to grasp my prey. My long sleek powerful wolf body was tense with anticipation and my black wings now immobile, stretched horizontally, the momentum already achieved for the final fast glide of my approach.

As I passed over the green, the witches ran shrieking in all directions and held up their arms in hopeless attempts to protect themselves. I could have plucked any one of them from the ground and ended their existence.

But they were not the target.

I was flying directly towards the huge bonfire where my prey was staring up at me.

My prey was the Devil.

The Fiend tried to twist away but was not fast enough.

The turbulent, buffeting air caused by my approach sent sparks from the fire whirling up into the sky. I felt a moment of ecstasy as my talons pierced his thick hide and gouged deep into the flesh of his back. He screamed as I bore him aloft.

I didn't soar upwards in a long spiral. My dark wings beat powerfully and I rose vertically, still gripping my prey. The Fiend was screaming, writhing and twisting, struggling to be free, but I held him fast, my talons biting even deeper.

This was what I was here on earth to do. My whole life had pointed towards this moment. Thousands of monks prayed daily against the power of the Devil and the forces of darkness. But I could do better than that!

This was *my* prayer! I was about to tear him to pieces and let him fall from the sky like shredded leaves. But as I gripped evil in my talons, I suddenly knew exactly what to do.

I hovered perhaps thirty or forty feet above the church. Then I dropped the Fiend towards the pointy spire. He screamed again as his belly was pierced by its sharp point which immediately emerged from his hairy back.

Impaled and writhing in agony, the Fiend began to slide down, spraying droplets of dark blood onto the roof of the church.

Then I swooped again. This time the witches had good cause to run and flee. As I flew low from north to south over the green, I slew some with my talons, ripping and tearing. One, a dapper little man wearing a white shirt, I seized and dropped into the flames. Then, before the remainder of the witches could flee the green, I attacked again, this time from the west. Many more of my enemies died.

Only as I completed my second sweep of the green did I realize that my attacks had been in the shape of a cross, that ritual sign that my brother monks made on finishing a prayer.

Soon the shrieking ceased and the green was deserted, the survivors having fled into the trees or back streets of the village. Now only Tom, Alice and the girl remained, gazing at me in astonishment, perhaps too stunned to truly appreciate their survival.

I gained altitude again and continued to watch from high above, again no more than a speck in the darkness. Tom limped towards Alice and began to unbind her, removing the gag from her mouth and freeing her from the silver chain which he handed to the girl. Then Tom enfolded Alice in his arms and hugged her. At last, he held her at arm's length and stared into her eyes. His face was badly bruised and one of his eyes was swollen.

They started to speak to each other. I was too far away to distinguish the words but it was clear that they were happy to be safe and reunited.

I reduced my size and landed some distance away from the fire, hidden from them by darkness. I was weary and I just wanted to lie down and sleep. It took all my strength to remain upright but I wanted to hear what they were saying.

'I tried to contact Wulf,' Alice said. 'I thought I'd failed. I was resigned to death but then I suddenly knew. Did you feel it, Tom, just as they were about to thrust us into the fire?'

'Yes,' Tom replied. 'There was a strange silence. I felt that something was about to happen.'

'That was exactly it! There's sometimes a moment, ain't there, when a silence falls over a forest?' Alice said. 'A second when the breeze halts and the leaves and branches no longer move: a time when every small animal keeps very still in fear and anticipation as if the very forest is holding its breath. And it happened then. I knew that something was approaching. I hardly dared to hope but knew it might be Wulf, didn't I? But never dreamed that he'd do *that*,' Alice said, shaking her head and glancing up towards the spire. 'How do you feel, Tom? You've taken a terrible beating . . .'

'I'm all right, Alice,' Tom said. 'I'll live to fight another day but now we need to get clear of here before some of those witches come to their senses. No doubt they'd like to repay us for what's just happened here.'

Alice nodded. 'Your poor face!' she said, staring at the girl.

'What if our way is still blocked?' the girl asked, ignoring Alice's comment.

'The way will be open now. Drawn the power to do that from the Fiend, they did,' Alice explained. 'Their ceremony failed and now he's been driven back to the dark with his stinky tail between his legs and so the spell will have collapsed.'

I looked upwards to the spire. Alice was right. The Fiend had already vanished. He'd gone back to Hell for sure, his followers scattered and forced to flee. Lit by moonlight, the only evidence that he'd ever been there the drops of blood scattered across the church roof that had sprayed from his wounded body.

'Then it's best if we take the route through Ormskirk,' Tom said.

'What about your bag?' asked the girl. 'Want me to go and get it from the inn?'

Tom shook his head. 'It's not worth the risk, Jenny,' he said. 'Everything in that bag can be replaced and I've still got the chain. Right, let's be on our way . . .'

I knew that once Tom would have had a special tinderbox in his bag, the one given to him by his father who'd died long ago. It was of great sentimental value and Tilda had once told me that he now thought it too precious to carry with him. Everything in the bag now had a replacement waiting back in the Chipenden house.

It was time to show myself. I changed the sky wolf for a human tulpa, this time not the boyish one that Tilda preferred. I selected the one designed to intimidate and fight my enemies.

It was the warrior tulpa and now I wore a dark cloak with the hood down across my shoulders, the front of it open to show my armour – a mail shirt that came below my waist. I had a sword in a sheath on my back and across my chest were leather straps with an assortment of blades of different sizes – I'd copied that from Grimalkin. As Brother Halsall, back at the abbey, used to say as he showed noviciates the work of older monks skilled in calligraphy: 'Learn from the best and then *become* the best!' It was good advice.

I walked towards them across the green, trying to inject energy and confidence into my weary stride. But that attack had taken a lot out of me. I was a bit shaky and would have loved to lie down, curl up and sleep until dawn.

'Hello, Alice. Hello, Tom,' I said, coming to a halt directly before them. 'And who's this?' I asked, looking at the girl.

I had hoped that Alice would greet me in the same friendly fashion, perhaps even thanking me for saving their lives. But she did neither.

'Where is Tilda?' she snapped angrily. 'Where is my daughter?'

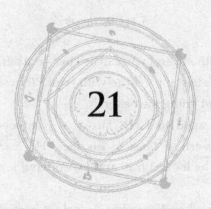

21

NOTHING TO FORGIVE

'Tilda is in Hrothgar's house, in his underworld,' I said. 'I think we should go there now. The journey will be shorter and far safer than travelling towards Chipenden. They're bound to come after us.'

'Why have you and Tilda stayed away so long?' Alice asked angrily. 'Do you hate me that much?'

'If I hated you, Alice, I wouldn't have helped you just now.'

Alice was no longer the young woman that I remembered. Her hair was white and there were lines round her eyes. But she held herself erect and hadn't even half an inch of spare flesh on her. Her back was straight and her eyes were sparkling with intelligence and energy.

Alice nodded, probably aware that she was being unfair, and gave a big sigh. 'I ain't ungrateful. Thanks for saving us, Wulf. Is Tilda all right?'

'Come with me and you can ask her yourself,' I said.

'I think it's best if we do go with Wulf,' Tom said, 'and the sooner we get going the better.'

Tom had aged too. His face was weather-beaten and there were vertical lines in his face. His back was also straight but he looked frail and I wondered if he'd been ill recently.

Without further discussion, we set off immediately and I took the lead. Our pace was slow because Tom was still suffering the effects of that beating. He staggered a couple of times, so Alice walked alongside him and put his arm across her shoulders by way of support.

Although somewhat slow, our progress was steady enough and Tom refused each offer of a rest. We passed north of Ormskirk before Alice sniffed out the first hint of danger. By then I'd led them away from the main track and into a forest. I preferred a more devious route away from prying eyes.

'There are witches behind us and something else directly in our path,' said Alice after sniffing the air. 'More than one of them – some sort of large animal, but nothing easy to identify.'

I didn't get a chance to explain as Alice set off again immediately. Then, just moments later, as we were crossing a clearing, there was a noise ahead of us and something burst through the undergrowth and ran straight towards me.

There were three of them altogether: large grey-furred creatures running on four legs, jaws open wide, fangs gleaming in the starlight, eyes glowing like molten rubies. But I wasn't afraid. It was Blood, Tooth and Claw, my tulpa wolves that I'd left guarding the gate. Soon after locating Alice, I had summoned them and they had hastened towards me. And now they were here just in time to do my bidding once more.

I knelt and opened my arms wide. In seconds they were on me, trying to lick my face, and I was patting them.

'It's all right, Alice. They belong to me,' I explained. Then I pointed west, directly behind us, and the wolves howled in unison before bounding away into the trees.

'They're tulpas that *you've* created?' Alice asked. 'Or do they belong to Hrothgar?'

'Yes, they're mine but aren't wraiths. They're *gristles* – something that I promised myself I'd never make but it proved necessary. But at least they aren't aware of what they are and can never suffer the anguish of human tulpas when learning the truth about themselves.'

'What made you change your mind?' Alice asked, her eyes suddenly wary. 'Last time we talked you were dead set against doing that.'

'I'll tell you later, Alice, when we take a rest. Let's just be sure the problem behind us has been dealt with first.'

Soon, there were noises to the west. They were too distant to hear clearly but I thought I heard a howling again and then several screams. When the wolves returned, there was blood on all three of their muzzles. Once more I patted them in thanks then sent them off again with a new task. We needed to eat.

Half an hour later we made camp, foraging for wood while Tom built up the fire and got it lit. I went out alone to greet the return of the wolves. They'd brought back the food as I'd bidden them to do – rabbits with broken necks but not a scratch upon them. First, helped by the nervous girl, who told me her name was Jenny, we gutted the animals while Alice improvised spits and positioned them over the fire. Tom offered to do the cooking but Alice brushed that aside.

'I can do it better and fussy I am over what I eat,' she said, smiling at him.

'There isn't enough for us and the wolves,' Jenny said.

'No need to worry. They've eaten already,' I told her.

So had I although I was still hungry. When I'd gone out to meet the wolves, I'd changed into the form of Black Fang so I'd eaten a large portion of the rabbits they carried, raw. Already I felt my strength being renewed.

We sat close to the fire and ate the cooked rabbits. Once we'd finished, Tom struggled to his feet. 'We need to get on our way as soon as possible . . .'

Afraid for Tilda, I felt like pressing on too, but Tom was close to exhaustion and when Alice spoke I couldn't bring myself to contradict her. If time had raced ahead in the outer world, only moments would have passed within the underworld.

'No, Tom,' Alice said. 'Nothing dangerous around at the moment. Best sit down and rest your weary bones for a while. Besides, I think Wulf should tell us what's wrong.'

'Wrong?' asked Jenny – I had been introduced now, but couldn't quite understand how she had reappeared, as I knew the girl had died many years go.

Tom sat down again. 'Yes, there's something badly wrong and I know that Tilda's part of the problem. So I want Wulf to stop holding back and tell us the truth.'

I nodded. 'I wanted to save you from this until we got back to the underworld but as you want the truth now, here it is . . . When we get back to Hrothgar's house, he won't be there and I've no means of contacting him. I think that he's probably dead. But what's even worse as far as you're concerned is the situation that Tilda's in . . .'

'You told me she was all right!' Alice protested.

'No, I didn't, Alice. I said she was back at the house.'

'You implied it. I ain't a fool! You didn't say anything was wrong, did you?'

'As I said, I wanted to save you the bad news until later—'

'Spit it out now!' Alice said angrily.

'When we get back to the house, you'll be able to talk to Tilda. But you won't be able to see her. And I think you're the only one who can do something about that . . .'

So I began my account of what had happened, leaving nothing out. The three of them listened in silence, not interrupting even once. I kept glancing at Alice but I could read nothing in her face.

At last, I brought it to a close. 'You see, Alice,' I explained, 'we didn't mean to stay away so long. The moment that Tilda became trapped behind the door her magic, which had been controlling the passage of time, no longer worked. Inside the underworld time changed so that in an hour, many years passed outside. And now when I return after about a day's absence, no more than a minute or so will have passed within. I'll have returned almost immediately as far as Tilda is concerned. How much time *has* passed by?' I asked.

'Nearly thirty years, give or take a few weeks. It's that long since you last visited Chipenden.'

I looked at her in astonishment. It was even worse than I'd guessed. 'But Tilda has been trapped behind that door for less than a day . . .'

'It might have been the reaction to Tilda's spells that matched inner to outer time,' said Alice. 'Once released from the spell the underworld raced away to compensate.' I breathed out hard; I had thought that might happen, but I hadn't expected quite such a long time to have passed. 'That can happen with such places – ain't stable, are they?' Alice continued. 'I'm sorry, Wulf, for all those years my anger grew.

I thought you'd just abandoned me and Tilda's father,' she said, nodding towards Tom. 'Please forgive me,' she asked.

'There's nothing to forgive,' I replied. 'It's only natural that you felt the way that you did.'

'Well, once within the underworld, I should be able to balance time just as Tilda did. The real problem will be to get her back from behind that door.'

'And to stop things coming through,' said Tom.

I nodded towards the wolves which were sitting together a little away from the fire. 'I made six of those creatures in all,' I said. 'I left the other three behind to guard the door. Whatever the threat, Hrothgar thought that gristles such as those would be effective.'

Within five minutes we were on our way again. We travelled all through the night and at about eleven in the morning we reached the two tall sycamores and I led them through into the invisible gateway into the underworld.

The wolves went off into the trees while the eyes of Alice, Tom and Jenny darted everywhere, taking in the red sky and the steps leading up to Hrothgar's impressive mansion with its unusual tall doors.

Once within, I led them directly to the library and beyond it down the passageway to face the locked door.

I called Hide, Hair and Bone away from the door and then moved very close to it and shouted out Tilda's name loudly.

There was no reply. I tried several times and fear clutched at my heart. I remembered what had happened to Hrothgar and feared for her. I turned away and faced Alice.

'Tilda's not replying. Open the door, Alice.'

Alice walked forward, a determined expression upon her face. She placed both of her hands against the door and muttered words under her breath. After a moment she stepped back and stared at the door and she spoke again. Her voice was a little louder this time but some of her words were still indistinct. There were also a few short phrases in Latin, a language which I remembered from my studies at the abbey. Priests used Latin in their prayers but I knew that witches often used the words from that language in their spells too.

Alice moved closer to the door again and she placed not just the palms of her hands but also her forehead against the wood. This time the words went on even longer – was she trying a different spell?

It was no good. Alice attempted to open the door several more times, her efforts continuing for almost an hour, but finally she had no more success than when I'd used my tulpa, Saint Quentin.

Tilda was still trapped behind the door.

22

THE ROOM OF CAGES

'I was afraid this would happen,' Alice said, burying her face in her hands. 'My magic's become weaker over the years. It's not strong enough to deal with something so difficult. This is what I've dreaded with every step of our journey here . . .'

'You tried your best, Alice,' I told her. 'I failed too. The magic binding the door is just too strong.'

I was trying to be supportive, but inside my fear and desperation were growing. My anguish at the lack of a response from Tilda had been temporarily held at bay by Alice's attempts to open the door. The thought of getting inside had helped me cling to the hope that it might not be too late to help Tilda. But now I was close to despair.

'There is one other way . . .' Alice said suddenly, staring at Tom. 'I could ask Pan for help.'

'No, Alice! Anything but that!' Tom said, and there was an expression of alarm on his face that I'd never glimpsed before.

I knew that Alice was an earth witch who had served that god of nature before. It was Pan who'd helped Alice escape the dark when she'd once been trapped there.

'What terrible price will Pan ask in return for his help this time?' Tom asked.

'Whatever it is, that price must be paid,' said Alice, her face filled with determination. 'This is our daughter we are trying to save. Don't forget that, Tom! No price is too high!'

Of course, Alice got her way and we left the mansion and went down the steps and into the trees. The three tulpa wolves guarding the gate came running towards me and I kept them close while, with a gesture that we should stay back, Alice went further into the trees alone.

As we watched her, Alice suddenly fell to her knees. Jenny gave a small gasp.

'I don't like this,' Tom said. 'Pan is usually benign but the price he sometimes demands for his help is extreme. He has little care for human feelings.'

Tilda had told me a little about what had happened in the past. As a price for releasing Alice from the dark, Pan had demanded that she work with and serve the mage called

Lukrasta. That had meant that for a time Alice and Tom had been forced apart. The Spook could not forgive the god for that, Tilda had said. I wondered if Tom thought that something similar would be the price demanded now.

Then there was another scary feature of Pan. He had dual aspects. At times he was a gentle boy, playing his pipes and surrounded by the creatures of the forest. At other times he was huge, terrible and powerful, creating dangerous storms and eruptions of the earth that caused devastation and untold human deaths.

Alice was quite some distance away but, illuminated by the baleful red glow from the sky, I could see her kneeling on the grass, her hands held high in supplication. Then she began to cry out so loudly that her words echoed through the trees.

'Pan! Pan! I beseech thee! Give me my power again! All of it! One last time! One last time! Please! That's all I ask. One last time before I die! In return, I will pay *any* price that you demand. I will do *whatever* you demand!'

I wondered if Pan would ignore her. If there was no service that she could perform, if he needed nothing, why should the god bother to respond?

But respond he did. There was no flash of lightning, no disturbance of the air, just a very faint sound of distant reed pipes being played, a sweet magical, haunting music that lingered upon the air and sent shivers up and down my spine. Soon that faded away but Alice did not move for a long time. She remained on her knees, her forehead touching the ground.

At last, Alice came to her feet and walked slowly back towards us.

'He did what I asked, Tom. My magic is strong again – at least for a while. He didn't say for how long . . .'

'And the price?' asked Tom, a haunted look in his eyes. 'What did he ask for?'

'He didn't tell me, Tom. No doubt he'll let me know when he wants something.'

Alice led the way back into the mansion, while I thought about what she'd just said. To have her magical power restored was good, but the debt she owed might be a price that could change her life for the worse. Tom's life too. He might be the one hurt most of all.

What might Pan demand in return? Tom's expression was bleak and I could tell that what had just taken place had badly shaken him. Obviously, he wanted his daughter returned safely but he would also fear losing Alice who was the love of his life.

Alice went straight to the locked door and gestured towards the three wolves. 'Keep them at a safe distance, Wulf. Tilda could be unconscious and close to the door. I don't want to risk hurting her so I'm going to force it to open outwards. Towards us.'

I whistled the three tulpas to my side and then, instead of moving closer, Alice took three steps backwards, creating more space between her and the door. Then she raised her left hand and began to chant.

I could feel the magic tingling in the air, which shimmered, making the door appear to distort. Seconds later I knew that it was not an illusion. It seemed that the only way to force the door open was to destroy it. Remembering how both Hrothgar and Tilda had opened it, and then been trapped when it shut behind them, it was obvious too that this was the best course of action. Suddenly it twisted, bulged and then – with a loud *whoosh* – exploded outwards into hundreds of fragments which then became small particles of wood and pieces of metal which fell at the feet of Alice. The door had been reduced to a heap of dust.

Beyond the door frame I could see only darkness. I wanted to lead the way in, but before I could move or call out Alice stepped inside. I quickly followed her.

Tilda was lying on her back with her eyes closed but I could see her chest rising and falling. She was breathing and still alive. A tremendous sense of relief washed over me, but I was still alert for danger and took in every detail of our surroundings.

The passageway was just as Tilda had described it, with torches in brackets on the walls. There was a high ceiling above and a narrow passageway, with about twelve feet of grey flagstones, leading to another identical tall door.

But there was one significant change.

That door was slightly ajar and torchlight flickered beyond it too.

'Help me carry her,' said Alice, who began to raise Tilda by the shoulders. I gripped Tilda's legs and we carried her back through to where Tom and the girl were waiting and I indicated the way to Tilda's room. Once there, after examining her, Alice rooted around inside the small pouch of herbs that she always had with her. She placed a small leaf under Tilda's tongue. Then she sent the girl Jenny for water and began to bathe Tilda's face and arms.

'Will she be all right?' I asked.

'I think so,' said Alice. 'Had some sort of shock, she has. Her heart was fluttering but it's now steady and strong. I think it best if you all leave the room for a while and leave me to tend her.'

We did as she asked. Then I spoke to Tom.

'The other door at the end of the passage was open. I'd like to see what's beyond it . . .'

Tom Ward nodded. 'You're right. We should check there for danger,' he said.

Before we left Tilda's room, I had picked up Tom's staff from where it was leaning and now I handed it to him. 'Thanks for lending it to me. Sorry I kept it so long,' I told him.

'Better late than never!' Tom said with a grin. 'My other one is broken so this will be very useful.'

The three of us went back to the library, but first I commanded the three tulpa wolves to stay and guard the door.

I left the wolves in their usual position, then we entered the passage again, the wall torches igniting as we walked towards the far door.

I eased the door wider cautiously and we stepped into a large room which contained something that I'd never suspected.

It was full of large metal cages, the door of each one fitted with a padlock. Inside each spacious cage was a dormant gristle. Some were lying down; others were upright as if ready to move at a command. There were thirty occupied cages because I counted them carefully. Some were creatures, ranging in size from a bear to a fox. About half of them were human in form and some were identical to ones I had met in various parts of the mansion. The ones standing were immobile, frozen into unconsciousness but with their eyes wide open as if awaiting the word of their master to awaken.

It was strange. Why had they not disintegrated like the others in Hrothgar's house and beyond? Were some of these creatures duplicates? They had to be because in one of the cages was Martha, the tulpa who'd lived in the cottage beyond the sycamore gate and shopped for us in the village.

But it couldn't be that *same* Martha because I'd visited the cottage and, after Hrothgar was taken, I'd seen the remains of her – just a heap of clay and dust on the floor.

But why had Hrothgar needed duplicates?

Then Tom pointed something out that I'd already noticed. In addition to the thirty that were occupied, there was an empty cage and the door was open. There was dried blood on the floor in front of it.

'The door's been forced!' Jenny said. 'You'd have to be incredibly strong to do that.'

The metal bracket holding the padlock had been bent and sheared off. Had the creature that had escaped from that cage been the one sniffing at the door when Tilda was trapped? If so, where was it now?

Then I noticed another black wood and metal door in the corner of the large room. It was identical to the others. Where did that one lead?

We needed to get Alice and let her see this.

Later, after we'd eaten, I went back to that room of cages with Alice. She left Jenny and Tom tending Tilda, who was still not awake, although Alice was confident that she'd make a full recovery.

Alice walked about the room silently examining each cage while I waited thinking things through. Slowly, but methodically, I had been arriving at certain conclusions and decisions. I now realized there was something that I had to do. I didn't *want* to do it but there was no way that my mind could wriggle free of that need.

When Alice had completed her inspection of the cages, together we walked to stand before the other locked door.

'I could open this door too,' said Alice. 'But doing that we'd risk letting something into this underworld . . .'

I stared at her. 'Are you sure?' I asked, already guessing what she meant.

'Yes, ain't no doubt about it. This is a doorway to the dark,' she said.

23

You Don't Scare Me, Witch!

'I need to go through that door,' I said, gazing straight into Alice's eyes.

'Why would you want to do such a stupid thing?' asked Alice.

'I need to find out what happened to Hrothgar. Because whatever did happen and whatever problem he tried to solve eventually might be my problem too. Do you remember me telling you how Hrothgar once saved my life during my early training?'

Alice nodded. 'You created something without intending to and it was trying to destroy you.'

'That's right, Alice. I'd thought I'd been dealing with saints that miraculously appeared out of thin air and helped me when I prayed hard, but I was wrong. I'd created tulpas without realizing it. One of them came out of the dark part of myself and Hrothgar helped me to destroy it. He told me that it was something that happened to every young tulpar, a crisis that we all went through. So, don't you see, Alice? This could be another type of threat faced by each tulpar after many years of developing the skills of their craft. Something that I might have to face one day. There's so much that I need to find out. What was in the empty cage?'

'Ain't that difficult to work it out, is it?' Alice said. 'It was another Hrothgar tulpa. One he struggled to control maybe. So it could be another bit of himself that either killed him or hurt him badly and dragged him off through that door into the dark!'

I nodded. Alice had arrived at the same conclusion that I had.

'So you do see why I need to find out what happened? I might have the same challenge one day. I need to follow them into the dark.'

'That would be madness,' said Alice.

'Crazy or not, it's something that I have to do. Will you come with me, Alice? You've been there before. And you've got your magic again. I was only in the dark once briefly while Grimalkin and Thorne killed Circe. Then they sent me back almost immediately. You know it better than I do. You could be my guide?'

Alice just stared at me, her expression full of hopelessness. 'I can't,' she said. 'Pan gave me back my magic but forbade me to ever enter the dark again in this lifetime. I'd like to help you, Wulf, but Pan is far more powerful than I am. I lack the strength to enter the dark. He's blocked it for me. I can't go there!'

'Then I'll have to go alone,' I told her.

'Go through that door and you'll be destroyed. And that destruction will be slow and infinitely painful. You ain't got a hope of success—'

'I have to try . . .' I told her.

Alice looked up at me. 'Don't you see, Wulf, that the second you step through that door the Fiend will know? It won't take long before he finds you.'

'I'll be ready for him.'

'Don't be a fool, Wulf! Don't be foolish and arrogant. Your sense of who you are and your capabilities has been exaggerated in your head by what you *think* you've achieved. You briefly bested the Fiend back in Churchtown because you took him by surprise. That was on earth, but to go through that door will be far different. The dark belongs to him. You ain't any hope at all of winning there where he rules and he'll enjoy gaining his revenge.'

'I've got to try. I'll fight him until I can fight no more.'

Alice laughed scornfully. 'He'll enjoy that. He'll play with you like a cat plays with a mouse. You create tulpas but that doesn't make you the equal of a god. Your own teacher, Hrothgar, who had a long span of time to develop his abilities, was defeated just a few steps beyond the edge of his own home. He hadn't even *entered* the dark! You've always been reckless and wilful and sometimes that paid off. But that wasn't in the dark. The Old Gods live there and draw their strength from it. You can't win there! Don't be a victim of your own delusions.'

I shook my head in disagreement and turned away, staring at the empty cage. 'Those who expect defeat are already defeated!' I told her. 'Those who bow to the strength of their enemies feed that strength. Maybe a touch of arrogance is just what I need?'

There was a long silence. When I turned back to face her, Alice's expression had changed and a little of the certainty had gone. 'As I've failed to change your mind, there are a few things I know that might help you,' she said. 'So listen carefully to what I say. The longer you stay in there, the weaker you'll become. Get out as soon as possible. And blood is the currency there. Everything that exists there needs blood. They'll take *yours* if they get the chance. But *you* can't afford to drink any blood or eat anything at all or you'll be trapped in the dark forever. If you can find water, you can drink that but that's all . . .'

'When you were in there, Alice, how did you survive?'

'Growing steadily weaker, I was. Every hour that you stay in the dark while alive, a little more of your life force fades away. Stay too long and that's the end of you. Even if you did manage to stagger back out into our world, you'd be nothing but a dry husk and would die within a few days. I wouldn't have got out but for Pan. The only way out for you would be to find your way back to this door.'

I nodded. 'I can't go until I've spoken to Tilda.'

'No harm in talking and saying your goodbyes, but don't try to persuade her to go with you, or you'll have me to answer to!' Alice warned me, her face clouding with anger. 'She'd be more at risk than you. Her blood is special as you well know. They'd sniff her out and be after her the second she stepped through that door. They'd be fighting each other to drain her.'

'I wouldn't want to take her into danger, Alice. Don't worry about that.'

'In that case you won't mind if I speak to my daughter first, in private?' asked Alice.

'Of course not,' I replied.

I had no intention of risking taking Tilda into the dark with me, but I did worry what else Alice might say to her.

I slept through what passed for night in Hrothgar's underworld. I did not dream although I knew that nightmares must be lurking in the corners of my mind.

I awoke, washed and went into the kitchen. I'd just finished eating when Alice walked in.

'How's Tilda?' I asked.

'She's awake and a lot stronger,' Alice said. 'She's waiting to talk to you now.'

Before reaching her room I changed the warrior tulpa for the shape of the boy, Wulf. I found Tilda sitting up in bed, a plump pillow at her back. She smiled at me, patted the bed and I sat on it, facing her as best I could.

'Don't go,' she said.

'I have no choice, Tilda. Did your mother tell you why I need to?'

Tilda nodded. 'It may never happen. You are Wulf, not Hrothgar. His problem could be a result of bad decisions that he made in the past. You might never face the same threat.'

'I might and I might not, but I can't take that chance. I have to know more about what Hrothgar did. That way I'll learn more about myself.'

'So I can't change your mind?'

I shook my head.

There was a long pause then Tilda nodded. 'Don't you think it strange, Wulf, how you reached Tom, Alice and Jenny just in time to save them from death in that fire?'

'I'd quite a few hours to spare,' I told her with a smile. 'I arrived long before sunset. The moment of danger didn't happen until midnight.'

'You're not thinking it through, Wulf. When I was trapped behind that door and my magic failed, time raced ahead in the outside world. In the hours before I sent you to get my mother, nearly thirty years passed in the outer world of the County. Yet you arrived just in time to save them. You could easily have been years too late. Or you might have arrived in the County years earlier. How do you explain that?'

I shrugged. 'I don't. I can't. One possibility – but it's unlikely – is that someone or something intervened so that I *was* just in time. Someone who wanted us to defeat the Fiend.'

'But who would be able to do that and why?'

I shrugged. 'It's just a possibility, that's all. And sometimes strange things happen anyway. It's as if some things are just meant to be!'

Tilda nodded. 'Those words are very true. Some things *are* meant to be . . . and I have something important to say to you. It's not just because of what you've decided about going into the dark. I've been thinking this way for a while, but seeing my mother and father so old has brought things to a head.' Tilda bit her lip, looking upset. 'There's no easy way to say this . . . but we need to part ways, Wulf. My mother and father need me. They need help in their old age. I can do my best to keep them happy and comfortable, and also defend them against the dark. They'll need it, as they age further and become less able to defend themselves. I'm so sorry.'

I stared at Tilda, hurt and confused by what she'd just said.

'I understand you want to help your parents, Tilda, but we can still see each other, can't we? I can visit you at the Chipenden house. Spend time with you there. I could help as well. I'm only too happy to do that.'

Tilda shook her head firmly. 'I've thought long and hard about it, and I really am thinking of both of us when I say this. I don't want you to see *me* grow old, Wulf. I don't want to watch your face as it happens. Eventually, I'll become shrunken and shrivelled, no longer the girl that you love now. You have the potential to live forever – not that I think you will: you take too many risks and I know that you'll eventually take one big risk too many, fight something that cannot be defeated. In that case I might even survive longer than you, Wulf. And that's something else that I can't bear. I can't face that hanging over me. As we just said – some things are just meant to be. I feel this is one of them. I've made up my mind, Wulf. And although it hurts both of us I intend to stick by that decision.'

My heart felt like lead. I couldn't believe that she'd reached this conclusion. Tilda had given me no hint previously of what she was telling me now.

'So eventually I'll go back to Chipenden to be with my parents,' Tilda continued, 'but I'll wait here for a while for your return and keep the passage of time between here and the outside world stable and the same, as long as I'm here. I'll be here waiting if you do manage to return from the dark.

I want to know that you're all right. But then we will have to part.'

'I can see you've thought all this through carefully,' I snapped.

'I have. Will you do as I ask? Will you do it for both our sakes?'

'I don't think it will be much for my sake. You're thinking more of yourself than me,' I said bitterly, 'but if that's what you want, how can I refuse you? It's your right to make that decision.'

Then we held each other close. We both wept.

When it was time to go, Tilda did not accompany me to the door. There was only Alice there to say goodbye.

I pushed my new sorrow to the back of my mind, trying to be optimistic. When I came back, I would work hard to change Tilda's mind. Surely she couldn't mean for us to part forever? In time I felt sure that she would relent.

Rather than ask Alice to use her magic, on impulse I took on the shape of Saint Quentin and placed my hand against the door. There wasn't the slightest hint of resistance. It opened outwards.

I returned to the shape of the boy tulpa and turned to Alice with a triumphant smile at what I had accomplished.

'Don't be too pleased with yourself,' Alice said with a sigh. 'Maybe those beyond that door wanted it to open.

Only too pleased to watch you enter the dark, they'll be. I'll need to strengthen it when you've gone. When you return it'll open for you but nothing else.'

Suddenly I felt a surge of anger. Was it Alice who had persuaded Tilda to break us up? It seemed that way to me. 'I can't leave without telling you a few home truths, Alice!' I snapped at her.

'What might they be?' Alice snapped back, her eyes glittering with anger.

'You and Tilda argued a lot and I know it was sometimes about me,' I told her. 'I know it was partly Tilda's fault that things didn't go more smoothly. After all, it takes two to argue. But she's younger than you and was just a young girl when the quarrels started. But you are her mother, Alice. You needed to be more tolerant. You needed to rise above it—'

'Take care what you say!' Alice warned. I could see the rage building within her but I couldn't stop myself. The words just poured out with the feelings that I'd kept bottled up.

'A mother should know when to let her daughter go, Alice! That's her final duty. Her final and most important gift to her child. But you couldn't do that, could you? What threat did you think I posed to Tilda? We loved each other. We were just like you and Tom!'

'I've reached the limit of my patience, child! One more word and—'

'And what? If that's what you think I am, then it's you who are deluded! I'm a *child* no longer. You don't scare me, witch!'

She raised both hands above her head as if to cast a spell at me but I just smiled. No doubt it was more like a grimace twisting my face.

Then I moved towards the open door and stepped out into the dark.

Before I'd taken three steps, I heard Alice slam the door shut behind me.

Immediately, I became the little dog with the thin rat's tail.

I became Piddle, the mongrel stray that everyone wanted to kick.

24

DEMON BLOOD

The first thing I noticed was that the sky was black, but just above the horizon there was a large full moon the colour of blood.

I was crossing a damp field of long grass, briars and nettles. There were lots of interesting smells, many of which I couldn't identify. I was curious. The dog part of me wanted to follow each one to its source. But I could see lights ahead and I kept moving towards them until I came out of the shadows into a cobbled street which sloped upwards.

The cobbles were black and shiny, like cobs of polished coal, and on either side of me were terraced houses with candles flickering behind lace-curtained windows. And at a few there were pale faces peering out. Whether dead humans or something demonic, it was impossible to say.

One side of the narrow street was well lit by the blood moon. The other was in dark shadow. But the most interesting thing was the open drain which ran close to the houses on my left. A dark liquid was trickling down the slope towards me and I was delighted when my nose told me that it was old blood. I halted and sniffed the delightful coppery scent. Just in time I remembered Alice's warning, but it took all my will power not to lick a little of it up into my mouth.

Alice had said that blood was the currency here and that the dead needed to drink it if they wanted to survive long in the dark. But I was still alive. If I drank even one drop of blood or ate one morsel of meat, I would be trapped in the dark forever.

There were lots of dead people in the street, grey melancholic figures wearing tattered clothes who shuffled along with their eyes fixed on the ground. They gave off a slight smell of decay and rot which I quite liked, although I preferred the odour of blood. Most had the appearance of walking corpses with a few bearing the marks of a violent death with open wounds or pieces of their bodies missing.

I wondered why they were gazing at the ground. Did they fear to meet the eyes of anyone else? If, while staring at the cobbles, they saw me weaving between the legs of that dead multitude, none of them aimed a kick in my direction or reacted in the slightest way to show that they'd even noticed me.

As I walked up that street, I began to regret my quarrel with Alice. I should have controlled my temper and kept my mouth shut. I should have shown Tilda's mother more respect. But it was done and I could do nothing about it. When I got back I would tell Alice that I was sorry.

The street soon ended at a wider one and I could have gone right or left. I chose left because that direction continued upwards, the incline slowly becoming steeper. It seemed a good idea to keep climbing, to get as high as possible. I kept sniffing the air. I was searching for a particular aroma – the scent of Hrothgar.

Piddle's keen sense of smell gave me a sudden warning of a threat. There was something behind me: something distinct from the smell of decay and rot that emanated from the dead who walked these streets of Hell. The stink of my pursuer gradually grew stronger as it got closer. I deliberately didn't turn to look at the creature which stalked me. I wanted it to think that I was unaware of being followed.

I left the street quite suddenly, darting into a really narrow dark alley on my left. The backs of the houses had no windows and therefore no one to witness anything that might happen. The end of the alley was blocked by a high stone wall, forcing me to turn and confront my pursuer.

It was about three times my size. Its head and body were feline, the hide spotted white and brown; its face – particularly the jaws – reminded me of the large predatory cats that I'd seen depicted in illustrated books back in the scriptorium at the abbey. Such creatures often killed their prey by using their back legs to disembowel them. But it wouldn't be possible for it to kill me in that way, its very long legs not being suited to that purpose.

It had six in all. They were long and slender like those of an insect and, as it stepped delicately towards me, they quivered as if struggling to hold aloft that heavy muscular piebald body. But I think that quivering might have been more due to the excitement and anticipation of killing me. Because it surged towards me very fast, its jaws open to bite my head from my body.

But I was already leaping upwards to counter its sudden attack. My own jaws fastened upon its throat, bit deeply and I fell away carrying a mouthful of the creature with me. I remembered Alice's warning and spat it out immediately.

The predator was dead.

Of course, by then I was no longer Piddle. I was something larger and far more dangerous. I was Black Fang, the wolf wraith, although brother indeed to the six grey gristles that I had created.

Then I took on the shape of Piddle again, wagged my thin ratty tail, and left that alley, continuing in the same direction up the street where the dead still shuffled across the cobbles.

Suddenly there came to my keen nostrils the scent of someone that I recognized. It was not Hrothgar. It was that of Grimalkin, the dead witch assassin!

She had been slain long ago but remained powerful – powerful enough to visit the earth during the hours of darkness. She had helped Alice many times, and on my previous brief visit to the dark had returned me to Chipenden.

Perhaps she might help me now? Alice could not be my guide here but perhaps Grimalkin would? It was worth a try. I would ask her.

I continued to climb, following her scent. After a while, a large square building of black stone, the same material perhaps from which the street cobbles were fashioned, gradually reared up before me. Its large forbidding entrance had a portcullis and there were bars on the windows with hooded figures patrolling the outside. It seemed to me that it was some sort of prison, and my nose told me that Grimalkin was somewhere inside.

Was she a prisoner? I found it hard to believe that Grimalkin would have allowed herself to be captured and held within such a place. Her choice would be to die fighting.

Getting into the prison was easy. I changed form in an alley and, after making myself as small as possible, entered in the shape of the sky wolf tulpa – but a tiny version.

No larger than a flying insect, I flew through the open bars. Once inside, the difficulties really started. To find Grimalkin I needed to take on the form of Piddle and use his keen nose. The prison stank, layer upon layer of odours, mostly sweat, blood and excrement. Buried among that were the individual scents of each prisoner and the devil creatures that were their gaolers. Only the sensitive nose of Piddle had any hope of finding Grimalkin among all that.

But each time I took that form there would be a risk. The long corridors were patrolled by the dangerous gaolers and I could not take on the form for long in case it were spotted.

I did not fear being seized or hurt – I felt confident of being able to defend myself or evade capture. But once those who guarded the place became aware of an intruder, security would increase and my task would become much more difficult.

However, sniffing faster than my tail could twitch, I quickly discovered the whereabouts of the witch assassin. She was being held far below ground in one of the deepest and most secure of the dungeons. I reached it within an hour, despite the many obstacles, most of which could be bypassed in the form of a miniscule sky wolf. Only once, when faced with a huge door without bars, blocking a corridor, was I forced to risk being discovered and use the lock-picking skills of Saint Quentin.

Finally, I flew through the bars of her cell and immediately changed my form to that of the boy, Wulf, becoming not too different in appearance from when Grimalkin had last seen me. Although a couple of inches taller, I was dressed in my old habit with the addition of the cloak and hood of a spook's apprentice.

As I was in the shape of the tulpa closest to what I had once been, often vulnerable, afraid and far less confident than the warrior or the sky wolf, the sight of Grimalkin brought so low filled me with dismay.

She was alive but in a sorry state.

She was breathing hard with her eyes closed, but whether beaten unconscious or sleeping it was impossible to say.

Four heavy padlocked chains shackled her to the damp slimy wall. Two were forged of iron, the other two from a silver alloy, both substances that were extremely painful and damaging to witches. But Tom Ward had once told me that Grimalkin had trained herself to be resistant to both metals. Once she had even endured the use of a silver pin to help strengthen a broken bone. But even the padlocks were constructed of iron and silver. Her captors were taking no chances.

She was dressed in a few rags and lying in her own filth, with cuts, bites and bruises all over her body. One glance told me that someone had been feeding from her. As well as old scars and healing wounds, there were fresh cuts still dribbling blood.

It was strange to see Grimalkin a helpless prisoner without a necklace of bones and an array of weapons. The last time we'd been together was when she and Thorne had slain the evil goddess Circe. They had been a formidable duo. Thorne had been trained as an assassin by Grimalkin and they were very close. That bond had remained even after both of them were dead and now in the dark. Thorne had said that they were 'slayers of gods', which was very true. Immediately following that slaying, Grimalkin had used her power to return me to earth.

How had the witch assassin been brought so low?

'Grimalkin!' I called softly.

I didn't need to speak her name again. She opened her eyes and stared up at me.

'I sent you back to safety, boy,' she said. 'You are foolish to return here!'

She'd opened her mouth to speak, revealing her pointy teeth, but although stained red it was not by the blood of her enemies. It was her own blood which dribbled through her lips and dripped from the end of her chin.

'You should have stayed away,' she continued. 'Soon you will be chained here too and suffer as I do.'

I smiled down at her and searched for words to reassure her, but then I heard the ominous clumping of heavy boots, the turning of a key and the grinding of a heavy door upon flags. I was aware that someone had entered the dungeon behind me.

I turned to face the trio of gaolers who were standing there. All three were huge and bulked with menacing muscle, more beast than human. One of them was taller than his companions, but his flesh was covered in scales rather than skin and he had a beak in place of a nose. His mouth was wide and filled with needle-thin fangs and he wore blades in abundance, many in sheaths upon his body, one even twisted into the topknot of his greasy hair.

'I could not have wished for more,' he growled, 'than to be provided with such succulent boy-flesh and the sweet blood that flows within your arteries and veins, Grimalkin. I will dine and sup well tonight.'

'I thank you for bringing so many blades with you,' I replied, smiling up at him pleasantly. 'Grimalkin needs new weapons. Yours will suffice until we can find better . . .'

He gave a roar of anger and drew two long blades from his belt. 'I see by your costume you were once a monk,' he said.

He was right about that.

'I will enjoy devouring both your flesh and your soul!'

He was wrong about that.

I changed my shape again. Now I was the warrior tulpa. There was a rasp as I drew the sword from the sheath on my back. I spread my legs to achieve perfect balance and gripped it two-handed.

The warrior tulpa is much braver than I am in my usual human form. Although not as reckless as the sky wolf, he always fights aggressively and does not know the meaning of the words *retreat* or *defence*. When using any tulpa body, I can moderate its performance, often having to rein in behaviours that to my human self seem unwise. But I have learned to let the warrior fight according to his instincts, thus freeing his natural ability.

He always attacks. He is always fast. He is always economical.

No cut is wasted. No movement is redundant.

Three strokes of my sword ended the threat.

There was a lot of demon blood.

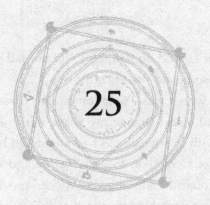

25

SWORD

When it was over, I briefly became Saint Quentin and freed Grimalkin from her shackles. Then, back in the form of the warrior, I gripped her by the arms and helped her to her feet.

'You risked much to return the favour I once did you,' she said with a smile which showed her pointy teeth.

'I didn't visit the dark specially to help you,' I confessed. 'I wasn't aware of your plight, but once you came to my notice I had to help because I owed you a lot. But now I would like to place myself in debt to you once again. I need your help.'

I opened my mouth to explain my need, but she gestured me into silence. 'Whatever your problem is, I will help,' she told me. 'I have already failed to come to the aid of one who I had promised to help when called – Alice scried me a message, but I could do naught. I will not fail you too. But first there is someone else we must free . . .'

I guessed who it was. 'Your companion, Thorne . . .'

Although I could change my shape and travel through the prison with relative ease, I had wondered how to make it possible for Grimalkin to find Thorne and then escape. But, even though I had witnessed it once previously, I had forgotten the astonishing things that this dead witch was capable of. She soon reminded me, changing into a shimmering orb no larger than a human head – the shape she habitually used to leave the dark and visit the earth. Then I realized how important the use of iron and silver had been to her gaolers. Not only did it confine her human form, but it had also prevented this transformation that would have allowed her to escape.

Neither did I need to find Thorne and take her to her companion's cell. Grimalkin led the way to her and, once Thorne was released, the three of us found it easy to escape the prison. In the shape of a small sky wolf, I followed the two orbs to a place of refuge. It was a small cave hidden high within the side of a steep hill and we made ourselves comfortable and gazed down upon the rooftops far below.

I gave a full account of what had happened. When I described how I had attacked the Fiend and impaled him upon the Churchtown spire, Thorne became very excited.

'Oh, Wulf! Wulf!' cried Thorne. 'You think and behave just like me. How I wish I could've done that. But perhaps I would have done more. I would have twisted my teeth deep inside his liver or perhaps bitten out one of his eyes! Do you know what Grimalkin once did to him?'

I could see by Grimalkin's face that she did not want this described, but she was like a tolerant mother with an enthusiastic, energetic daughter and had to let her have her say.

'Grimalkin carried the Fiend's head in a sack so as to prevent his worshippers re-attaching it to his body. She was taking refuge in Malkin Tower from a fierce horde of them who were gathered in a clearing gazing up at her. She drew forth the Fiend's head from the sack and stabbed the blade of her knife deep into his left eye. Then she threatened that unless they did her bidding she would take his other eye. It was truly marvellous!' Thorne cried.

'Calm yourself, child,' Grimalkin said softly, patting Thorne upon her shoulder. 'Yes, it is time to destroy the Fiend. That ugly hairy bestial god cannot be permitted to rule the dark again. But first we will give Wulf the help that he needs. I am intrigued by the mystery of Hrothgar's behaviour. It is something that we must solve together. But even if I were not, then I would still owe a great debt to Wulf.'

Her eyes locked upon mine. 'In saving Thorne and me you have done much more than the simple service I once performed in returning you to the County. Yes, we will solve your mystery and then, once that is done, we will deal with the Fiend.'

'I'll help you with that too,' I told her.

'Perhaps, but it depends how long our first task takes. You cannot stay too long in the dark. Your life force is being drained even as we speak. Soon your strength will start to ebb.'

I nodded. 'How can we best find Hrothgar – and the creature that carried him off?' I asked.

'They could be anywhere,' said Grimalkin. 'The dark is huge and has many domains. The town below us, and the area surrounding it, is the closest part of the dark to the earth, the place of the *downcast-dead*.'

'Who are they?' I asked.

'They are the dead who shuffle down those narrow streets afraid to meet anyone's gaze and draw attention to themselves. That town is where damned souls first enter the dark and they are the easiest victims for the many predators who gather there seeking fresh blood. But this is just one part of the dark. Although Hrothgar entered here, he could quickly have moved elsewhere. There are portals that permit almost instantaneous travel between domains. But there is one person that I can consult. He owes me for favours I have done him in the past. And he'll help us anyway once he hears my proposal . . .'

'The Piper?' cried Thorne.

'Yes, we will ask the Piper,' Grimalkin said.

We climbed the wooded hill behind the cave, moving directly away from the town below us and the blood moon, which never seemed to change its position low in the sky.

'I love the new shape that you have taken on, Wulf,' said Thorne, walking close beside me. 'I like tall men!'

I had become the warrior tulpa, ready for any dangers that we might face. Grimalkin was striding ahead, setting a furious pace. She wore the straps and blades of the tall demon that I had slain. I sensed that after her forced immobility she was eager for action.

'I wish I could take on shapes like you,' Thorne continued. 'Do you keep making new ones?'

'Yes, but I don't want too many. Each one serves a particular need or has a special skill. I'm wondering if Hrothgar brought this danger upon himself by creating too many tulpas.'

'Here we are!' said Grimalkin. 'This is the Mud Lake.'

It didn't look much like a lake to me but it was certainly muddy. We'd arrived at a large oval pond surrounded by trees and shrubs and encircled by tall reeds. The water was murky, the colour of mud, and of whatever lay beneath its surface, nothing was visible. But I felt uneasy just looking at it.

Grimalkin gestured that we should sit so I positioned myself on the ground and Thorne sat close to me. The witch assassin remained standing, then raised her arms so that her fingers were pointing at the dark sky. She began to chant.

Thorne grinned at me and stared at the water, tapping her fingers on her knees excitedly.

'Have you been here before and met the Piper?' I asked.

'Watch the water!' she exclaimed. 'Just watch!'

No sooner had I looked back towards the pond than its murky surface became agitated, ripples spreading from a point right at its centre.

A tall pointy wide-brimmed hat rose up before us. It was perched upon an elongated face with wide-open green eyes with pupils like those of a goat. The face was made to appear even longer by the white beard, and the mouth was downturned in disapproval, suggesting that the Piper was less than happy to see us. Despite that, Thorne was giggling, her eyes shining with delight.

The Piper was dressed in a long green gown, the sleeves of which came down to the tips of his fingers. He seemed to be standing on the surface of the water, but his feet and legs were not visible, the hem of his gown still submerged. His hat was dripping, but his upper body appeared remarkably dry for someone who'd just emerged from the depths of a pond. Whereas from his knees downwards his gown was coated with green slime.

'What do you want now, witch?' he said in a peevish voice which was far from welcoming. 'Once again you've disturbed my sleep!'

Thorne leaned across. 'He's always grumpy when he first wakes up but he has a heart of gold!' she whispered in my ear.

'We wish to be astonished by your excellent abilities. We desire your help in a very important matter,' said Grimalkin, her words flattering but her tone one of mockery.

'And what will be my reward?' asked the Piper.

'Your reward will be to assist us in a project that I believe is very dear to your heart . . .'

'And that is?' he asked, but he no longer looked quite so grumpy and unfriendly.

'Soon we intend to destroy the Fiend. Help us now and you may join us. I will allow you to play a major part in that enterprise.'

Now the Piper was actually smiling. 'You are so kind, Grimalkin!' he said enthusiastically. 'What other allies will join our cause?'

'There will be no further assistance. There will just be the four of us.'

'Just *four of us* against the might of the Fiend and his numerous supporters!' he said, his voice also full of mockery now. 'That is better than I could ever have dreamed. That will be a battle of truly heroic dimensions and is sufficient reward for anything that you care to ask of me, Grimalkin.'

'Well, I do not require anything that will tax you too much. All I need from you is the whereabouts of a creature named Hrothgar, who entered the dark very recently. He was probably the prisoner of another being almost identical to himself.'

'Very tall but proportionally thin, isn't he?' the Piper said. 'Yes, I was aware that he'd joined us in this most delightful place. But he was not a prisoner. He entered the dark alone. I don't know where he is now but I could soon find out. Is that all you want?'

'Yes. Find him and we will attend to the rest.'

'It will be done within the hour,' the Piper said. 'I have met your young and beautiful companion before,' he said, nodding at Thorne, who burst out giggling again. 'But who is the sombre warrior who sits beside her? I would know more about him.'

'My name is Wulf,' I told him. 'I was once a noviciate monk, then for a short while I became a spook's apprentice. Now I'm a tulpar.'

'Are you indeed? Such a varied career you've had, Wulf, a little like my own. Once I was a powerful mage – but in those ancient days I called myself a *wizard*. Then I commanded eagles but now I have to make do with rats . . .'

Something slid down his sleeve. He grasped it with his right hand and lifted it to his lips. Unlike the reed pipes played by Pan, this was a silver flute and he began to play.

Pan's music had been haunting, complex and melodic. This tune was simple, strident and rousing.

As he played, a large grey rat swam through the reeds and then climbed up onto the bank of the pond. It had a longer tail than Piddle and also longer sharper teeth. Within moments others joined it.

Soon the bank was swarming with rats. Then the Piper stopped playing and gave a guttural command in a language that was unknown to me. The rats ran away from the pond in all directions.

'They'll soon find Hrothgar,' said the Piper. Then he stared at me hard and frowned. 'Well, Wulf, you'll need a sword for the battle ahead. I think that I can provide one that you will find suitable . . .'

Puzzled by his words, I reached over my shoulder to draw my sword and show him his mistake. But my fingers gripped empty air. I was momentarily angered, knowing that he'd used some enchantment against me. After all, how could my sword go missing when it was an intrinsic part of the tulpa I called the warrior? It was an essential element of what I'd created using my imagination and innate abilities.

By now the Piper had reached down into the water as far as his elbow and seemed to be groping for something. When he pulled his arm back out of the water and raised it above his head, he was holding a sword covered in mud.

What a sword it was too. As the soft mud slithered from it, dripping into the water, its full magnificence was revealed. It gleamed from blade-tip to hilt like silver. Who could have believed that it had been buried in the mud at the bottom of the pond? There were inscriptions on the hilt too that looked like runes.

Then he threw it up into the air and caught it by the blade. The edge looked sharp and I thought he must have cut himself badly, probably to the bone, but when he held it out to me, hilt first, there was neither one drop of blood nor even the most superficial of cuts on his palm.

'Here, Wulf, take it,' he said with a smile. 'This weapon will serve you well. You won't be the first promising young man that I've loaned this sword to. For most it was the making of them!'

'You're very generous and I thank you for the offer but I can't take it,' I told him. 'A sword such as that, external to my being, would fall to the ground and be lost the moment that I change my shape.'

'That will be no problem. It's just a simple matter of calling the weapon to you once you're ready to receive it. Here it is. Take it now!'

I reached for the sword but it simply disappeared and he smiled. Once again, I was annoyed and thought he was using his magic to make fun of me for his own amusement. I glanced back at Grimalkin and Thorne but their faces hadn't even a hint of a smile or any indication that I was being mocked.

'Call it to you, Wulf! Call it by its name!' the Piper commanded.

I shook my head in annoyance. 'Then what is its name?' I asked.

'It's called Sword, of course! What else would you call it? Go on. Call it to you, using its name.'

Feeling foolish I called out, 'Sword!'

Instantly, there was a loud rasp and I felt the weight of the sword as it slid into the scabbard on my back.

'Now that wasn't too difficult, was it?' asked the Piper.

26

THE GRISTLE
DOPPELGANGER

Well before the hour was up, the rats began to return. Some paused briefly before the Piper and squealed before entering the pond. Others just splashed straight in.

Finally, there were no more rats. Grimalkin was pacing up and down on the edge of the reeds and I could tell from her expression that she was impatient.

'That's it,' said the Piper. 'My final rat has reported in.'

'Well?' she demanded. 'Have you found him?'

'Of course,' he said with a smile. 'Have I ever let you down? But it is not good news. Hrothgar is dying, but he's not that far away. He crawled into a cellar. But if we hasten, we may be in time to listen to his final words.'

'Is he still alone?' I asked. If so, that was very strange; all the evidence suggested that he'd been carried off by his double.

'Yes, he is still alone,' said the Piper. 'Now follow me or we will be too late . . .'

We followed him down the hill towards the town of the downcast-dead and predatory demons, with its narrow streets of black cobbles. I felt that we were no better than rats being summoned by his playing. But that was a little unfair. I realized that he meant well and no doubt he was leading us to Hrothgar. It was just something about his air of superiority that annoyed me, my feeling that he considered himself to be cleverer and better than we were.

The lower we descended, the narrower and darker the streets became until the blood moon was totally lost to view. At last, we entered the meanest and darkest of them all, a narrow cul-de-sac that ended in a wall with a square hole in the ground before it. There were stone steps leading downwards.

Like rats scurrying at his heels, we followed the Piper down into the darkness, but below it wasn't dark, not even gloomy. There was a warren of passageways lit by ample torches, each corridor ending in small flagstoned cellars without doors.

'It's one of many places here where the dead die a second time,' the Piper said, glancing over his shoulder and looking directly at me.

'And that second death brings oblivion,' said Thorne. 'The soul is permanently extinguished.'

The Piper halted and pointed to a doorway. 'He is in there, Wulf. Now you must lead the way.'

Grimalkin, Thorne and the Piper entered the cellar after me, but they then remained standing close to the door while I approached the still form of Hrothgar. At first glance I thought that I was too late and he was already dead because he was lying on his back completely immobile. He didn't seem to be breathing.

Lying on a pallet of straw, his long body appeared thinner than ever. Where the flesh was visible – on the face, wrists and hands – it was dry and sunken. The face had a grey pallor as if no blood flowed within and the eyes were closed. He seemed to be no more than a dry husk.

But suddenly he opened his eyes and twisted his head to look at me. Then he spoke a warning.

'I thought you had a good sensible head on your shoulders, Wulf. I'm surprised at your stupidity in entering the dark. Beware, Wulf. Look upon me and learn from this. Do not follow in my foolish footsteps . . .' His voice was little more than a dry croak and now he was certainly breathing but at great cost. He was struggling to draw air into his lungs, pausing to pant every few words.

'I find it hard to see you this way,' I told him. 'It saddens me. I owe you a lot, Hrothgar. You explained to me what I truly am and then guided me through the phase of my development that might have destroyed me. Is there anything that I can do to help?'

Hrothgar shook his head. 'It's too late for that, Wulf, but I would like to give you something – one last piece of advice that might enable you to avoid what has happened to me.'

'Where hides the creature that did this?' I demanded. 'Was it a tulpa that you created accidentally, or maybe some dark aspect of yourself? Am I correct? If so, I must find it and destroy it.'

'I did it to myself so there is nothing to hunt down, Wulf. Yes, I divided myself into good and bad aspects, but they are now united within me and cancel each other out. But their final coming together has brought about my destruction.'

'Then the creature in the cage *was* another part of yourself?'

'Yes, it was a gristle but this time against all sound practice animated by another splinter of my soul – one too many, I'm afraid. I tried to keep it safe and bound but it was too strong and escaped. Then, despite all my efforts to prevent such a thing, it merged with me and we became one. As I just explained, that violent forced unification is what has destroyed me. Thus learn from this, I beg you. Will you listen and learn?'

'Of course,' I answered.

'Then understand that you cannot create too many bound wraiths. Each time you do so your soul splinters, and once it has been divided too many times the potential for evil that is within us all begins to take over. Wrongness, pride, wilfulness – all the dark aspects of a human personality – start to become uppermost. But I tried to overcome it, Wulf. I cut away all those evil parts of myself and placed them within my double, the doppelganger of myself. This creature I locked away behind the black door within a cage where I hoped to confine it forever . . .'

'But why did you create it as a gristle?' I asked.

'It was the only way to ensure that I didn't use it by accident. A bound wraith is too accessible, like a person pulling on the wrong coat by mistake and realizing too late what they are wearing. But as a gristle that risk of an accident was eliminated. It was physically independent of me and could be caged.'

'As you caged the other gristles?'

'Yes, but there was no evil intention in that for those others, just expediency. In their cages they were dormant and had no awareness, and they were useful duplicates in case one of my servants was ended by accident as can happen over the long time that I have lived. Within that small space beyond the black door, no magic but mine could exist and all that I created was preserved from decay. Some were experiments too by which I developed my art and learned my trade. But my gristle doppelganger escaped its cage and was waiting for me. It drew me into its physical body so that we were joined. How I fought to escape, but gradually it grew stronger and that powerful evil aspect of myself could not be cast off again. I fought and fought but I lost the battle.'

'Were you joined with it even as you walked about the house and spoke to me? Was that why you couldn't touch Tom Ward's staff – because it's made of rowan wood?'

'Yes. When I asked you to carry it from the library, the struggle within me was reaching a crisis, and I wanted you and Tilda away from the door and the area beyond. I tried one more time to free myself from the gristle but it began to feed on my soul. In that struggle, I lacerated my flesh with my own hands. But as it fed, we both weakened and began a slow descent towards death. Then it carried what remained of me within it off through that door into the dark. I began to fight back again and still fight even to this very minute. I am dying but will take my evil aspect with me.'

'Why was your house built round that gateway to the dark?' I asked. 'Wasn't it an ever-present danger?'

'Of course it was. That was something that always needed to be guarded against. But that danger was exactly *why* I chose to build my home there. I was young and growing in power at the time. I felt it my duty to seal that gateway and keep out denizens of the dark. And for many long years I was successful. But then it was the fault within me that changed things. Take care that you do not suffer the same fate.'

'What you say is easy to understand on one level. So I will not splinter my soul too many times. I'll limit the number of bound wraiths that I create. But how many can I create with safety, Hrothgar?'

'Each of us is different, Wulf. I cannot put a number on it. You must make that judgement for yourself. But your training as a monk might help. Think of the sins that your teachers in the abbey preached against – pride, envy, greed, sloth and many more. Some priests say there are seven deadly sins but, in truth, there are sins without number. Particularly be aware of the danger that you no longer care for other people's feelings and that you become selfish and wilful, only doing what *you* find pleasing. The sense of that growing within you is one sign that you are approaching the point when you could well splinter your soul one too many times . . .'

'But you have managed to defeat that evil part of yourself,' I said.

'It is as strong as I am and tries to stifle my words even as I struggle to speak. If it could, it would reach out and slay you. So it is better that we die now together. Once it released what it was, it was doomed to disintegrate anyway, but the process has been slow.'

'I wish I could help you.'

Hrothgar did not reply. He just shook his head and gave a deep sigh then and closed his eyes. I stayed with him for a long time until I became aware that he was no longer breathing.

Then, as I watched, the gristle tulpa that had housed both Hrothgar and his doppelganger began to dissolve and collapse into a long heap of dust and decay.

He had died the second death.

We returned to the cave far above the town, leaving the Piper behind. Grimalkin told me that he would find us when we were ready to move against the Fiend.

Back in that cave I was restless and eager to get on with it. I could feel myself growing weaker. I could not afford to stay in Hell much longer.

'I want to help you to destroy the Fiend,' I told Grimalkin. 'But it must be soon. I don't want to become trapped here.'

'Before we do that, Wulf, I would like you to do one more thing. Visit Pan and tell him what we are about to do. Ask if he would aid our cause and be prepared to rule the dark if we are victorious. I would go myself, but he does not like anyone intruding upon his privacy. Thorne and I have done it previously and it would not be wise to repeat that offence.'

'Do you think he'll agree?' I asked.

'I doubt it because he values his own world and way of existence too much. But it is well worth asking him. Were he to agree, it would offer stability rather than the chaos that must ensue once we have destroyed the Fiend. If Pan joins his strength with ours, it will also greatly increase our chances of success. For despite my bravado when speaking to the Piper, what we attempt is fraught with danger. There is not only the Fiend to overcome but also those who serve him. Many of them are formidable indeed. But even if Pan does refuse he might offer us some help. Anything would be better than nothing.'

It seemed to me that I would be in danger going uninvited into Pan's domain. But what Grimalkin asked of me was well worth pursuing. In order to destroy the Fiend, we would need all the help we could get.

Grimalkin gave me a smile that showed her pointy teeth. 'When you speak to Pan, say that you are offering to help him become the deserved ruler of the dark rather than begging for his help. Even the Old Gods like flattery!'

In the shape of the sky wolf, I followed the two orbs that were Grimalkin and Thorne over a nightmare landscape of black bottomless pits. Below us were islands, each the domain of an Old God or a demon, and these were connected by white stone paths overhanging the deep dark abysses that separated such dwelling places.

When we came within sight of Pan's domain there was no mistaking it. It was larger than the other domains and of such verdant green that it dazzled my eyes. The baleful light of the blood moon above us did not reach it.

Here the two orbs halted, hanging immobile above the void, while I flew on alone to face Pan.

27

THE BONE FORTRESS

I landed on the grassy edge and immediately took on the form of the boy I had once been. Ahead of me was a forest, a thicket of saplings surrounding tall trees full of white blossoms.

It made me think of early spring but maybe it was always spring here. Pan was one of the Old Gods – he could fix his domain in the form that he best liked it.

I began to feel very nervous – and that quickly became fear. I knew that the word *panic* came from Pan's name, that a sense of dread was often felt as he drew near. But he had two aspects and that was when he was in his terrible wrathful shape. I was hoping to meet him as the benign boy who played reed pipes. Then, hopefully, he would listen to what I had to say.

I pushed my way through the thicket of saplings and entered the trees and it wasn't long before I could hear the sound of pipes. The haunting music was exactly as I remembered it from when Alice had knelt to him in the underworld.

I moved quickly towards it until I stepped into a clearing thick with green ferns. At its centre was Pan, surrounded by the creatures of the forest

Pan, in the form of a pale-faced fair-haired boy, was sitting cross-legged on the ground playing a reed pipe. His shirt and trousers seemed to be made out of leaves, bark, grass and reeds. The face was reassuringly human but the ears poking up through his long unkempt hair were very long and pointy. I couldn't help staring at the long green toenails of his bare feet, each one curling upwards into a spiral.

Surrounding Pan was a dense crowd of creatures charmed by his pipe; they all were intently watching him play. There were rabbits, hares, rats, mice, badgers, voles and tiny shrews while upon each shoulder was a squirrel, one red-furred and one grey. Hovering above his head and alighting upon his hair were hundreds of multi-coloured butterflies. A small black cat rubbed its head against his foot while, above Pan, the branches were bowed with the weight of birds. All were silent and still, held in thrall to the source of that exquisite music.

Without ceasing to play, Pan looked at me and gave a nod downwards towards the ground. I immediately understood that he was commanding me to sit before him. In that moment as he glanced at me, I'd seen a flicker of indifference, almost disdain, in his gaze.

Did he dislike me? Had this god judged me with a single glance?

What went on within the mind of a god? I sensed that although humans were part of the nature that he ruled, he did not hold us in particularly high regard. Or perhaps it was something else essential to his being?

As the god of nature, he must surely wish all life to thrive – but I suspected *individual* lives did not really matter. After all, nature was a great heaving upwards of lives, each one doomed to fall back, die and decay, only to be replaced by another. As long as squirrels perched upon his shoulders it was not important which ones. A dead creature could be replaced.

Those thoughts made me wary and a little anxious about how he might react to my visit. So I sat facing him at a respectful distance, watching him play the pipes, listening to that compelling music. At last he ceased playing and laid the pipes on the ground just in front of him. None of the creatures moved, but the birds on the branches above were no longer silent. They burst into harmonious song as if they were a trained choir performing for their god.

'You are many creatures in one,' Pan said to me. 'Take care that you do not become too many and lose yourself!'

This was what the dying Hrothgar had warned me about. It was that mistake which had brought about his own destruction. Each time I made a wraith, I splintered a piece of my soul away to animate it. How many times could you do that before you were in too many pieces and forgot who you really were? Hrothgar had not been able to give me a clear answer. It was not as simple as counting. But I knew that, above all, I must care for others more than myself. I must be selfless rather than selfish. That wouldn't always be easy.

'Why are you here?' asked Pan. 'Why have you entered my domain uninvited? What do you wish from me?'

'Forgive me for intruding without permission,' I told Pan. 'I came here uninvited because I wish to speak to you and knew no other way to make that possible. But I ask for nothing. I'm just here to offer you my help to become what you should be . . .'

'And what is that?'

'The ruler of the dark!'

Pan smiled mysteriously. It was impossible to tell whether it was a friendly smile or a mocking one or even that rare brief false smile – the dangerous tic of the face that seizes some people before they strike out at an enemy.

In the silence which followed, the small black cat ceased rubbing against Pan's foot and crossed the space between us. Without thinking I reached out my hand and began to stroke its head. In response it began to purr very loudly.

'And what help would you give me to become that?' asked Pan, staring at the little black cat.

'With the aid of Grimalkin, I will kill the Fiend,' I told him.

Some of the butterflies were hovering above my head now. One settled upon my left shoulder.

'Those are brave words, but even if you could make good that boast. I prefer to live in peace and attend to the things which concern me. To live in harmony with these creatures and to protect and care for them, that is all that I need.'

'With the death of the Fiend would come peace, allowing plenty of time for you to attend to what best pleases you.'

'I would never wish to become the ruler of the dark,' said Pan. 'Rulers come and rulers go. Things change and then return to the way they were previously. Even a god can be destroyed. I came close to that recently. I fought Golgoth, the Lord of Winter. My own narrow victory came at a price. It was not easy to regain my strength.'

'I'm sorry,' I told him, 'but I had to ask. We will try to kill the Fiend anyway.'

'Perhaps I can give you a little help. Take these . . .' He suddenly closed his right hand tightly, shaping it into a fist. Then held it out towards me.

I held my own hand beneath his, palm uppermost. He relaxed his own hand and a small cloud of seeds dropped into my palm.

'They might help,' he said with a smile. 'Seeds have potential. When you face the fortress of the Fiend, cast these upon the ground before his door!'

'Thank you for giving these to me. But I can't carry them – when I change my shape anything additional to the original tulpa falls away and is often lost.'

'All your tulpas have mouths, don't they?' he asked.

I nodded.

'Then there is the answer. But try not to swallow them – that could be most unfortunate! Are you thirsty?' he asked.

'Yes,' I replied. 'But I fear to take any sustenance from the dark in case I become trapped here.'

He smiled and suddenly there was a wooden goblet in his hand, which he held out towards me. It was brimming with a clear liquid. 'Take it and drink deeply,' he commanded. 'It is water and water is life. Drink and be filled with new strength.'

I thanked him and sipped from the goblet. It was cold and pure, like water from a mountain stream just below the snow line. I drained the rest and handed it back to him.

'Go now!' he commanded.

I bowed, then left Pan and walked to the edge of his domain. There I placed the seeds within my mouth for safe keeping. They had a bitter taste. I concentrated lest I swallow one and become doomed to stay in the dark forever. Then I changed into the form of the sky wolf and soared aloft to where the two orbs hovered, awaiting my return.

As I flew, I became aware that my weariness had completely gone and I felt as strong as when I had first entered the dark. So Pan had given me two gifts.

We returned to our refuge in the cave and Thorne and I stayed there for a short time while Grimalkin went off alone. She gave no reason for leaving and I did not ask.

I had wondered where the Fiend was to be found. Pan had mentioned a fortress so I asked Thorne about that as we sat together in the mouth of the cave staring down at the town of the downcast-dead, which was bathed in the red light of the blood moon.

'He'll be in the *Bone Fortress*,' she explained. 'It's where all rulers of the dark spend time, especially while they're gathering their power and making sure of their position. As he's only just become the ruler, he's certain to be there. He'll be holding feasts and trying to increase his support from demons and minor deities.'

'What's the Bone Fortress like?' I asked.

'It's not made of bones, if that's what you're thinking,' Thorne said with a smile, moving closer to me so that our shoulders were touching. 'It's built of black stone with high walls and lots of towers and turrets. But the front wall is almost totally covered with skulls – soon it will be full up and they'll have to start fixing them to the back wall or one of the side ones. They call it the *Skull Wall*. And that's where the only door is. We'll have to go through that to attack the Fiend.'

Suddenly I began to doubt our chances of success. 'Then it'll be well guarded?' I asked.

'Not at all,' said Thorne. 'No ruler of the dark would ever dream that anyone would attack them in their own lair. And the Fiend doesn't have much imagination – he's not like you, Wulf. He'll never consider for a moment that just four of us will go in that front entrance and try to destroy him. There won't even be guards there.'

'You make it sound easy!' I said, laughing.

I suddenly felt Thorne shiver against me. 'Getting in will be the easy part. The hard part will be fighting our way through to the Fiend. Once there we've got the problem of killing him. I often boast about how Grimalkin and I are the slayers of gods. Well, that's not empty talk because we've killed two goddesses so far. But this will be much more difficult. They were alone. The Fiend is stronger than either of them and will have hundreds of demons there to defend him.'

Grimalkin returned soon afterwards with news that there would be no further delay. A new feast was beginning at that moment, presided over by the Fiend in the large banqueting hall in the Bone Fortress. She had already informed the Piper and he would meet us there.

We were about to attack.

28

A GORY FEAST

We walked up the steps towards the great door of the Bone Fortress. It was a daunting place, its black towers reaching high into the sky. But its huge front wall, as Thorne had explained, was covered in skulls.

The colour of the Skull Wall was not shades of white, yellow or brown as I'd expected from a mixture of very old and relatively recent bones. It was bathed in the red light of the blood moon, making it seem as if those skulls had been dipped in blood.

Grimalkin was on my right, Thorne on my left. Both were well provided with blades which they wore on diagonal straps across their bodies. They also wore new necklaces of thumb-bones round their necks. They had been out hunting together – that was the result.

Behind us walked the Piper. He carried a long staff in his left hand and his silver flute in his right. His hair and beard were of such a brilliant white that it seemed to me that they cast our three shadows upon the ground ahead of us. But slime coated his gown from his knees downwards and he left a trail behind him like that of a snail.

At last we reached the flat area of stony ground before the door. While my companions watched, I spat the bitter seeds from my mouth onto the ground.

We all stared downwards but nothing happened. How could they germinate and root on such stony ground?

'All in good time,' said the Piper, as if reading my mind. 'With regard to the forces of nature, a little patience is sometimes required . . .'

But, even as he spoke, small green shoots erupted from the ground and formed thorny vines which began to snake through the stones in the direction of the Fiend's redoubt. It suddenly struck me that had I swallowed them, I'd have had more things to worry about than staying in the dark forever.

We walked on towards the huge door. 'I will deal with this,' said the Piper. 'I can usually get most of them open.'

I could have become Saint Quentin and unlocked the door myself, but I waited politely while he stepped forward and muttered something under his breath. Just as I noticed that on both sides of us the thorny verdant vines were climbing the wall at a remarkable speed, the heavy door slowly swung open, creaking upon its hinges. Beyond it was a dark passageway with nobody obstructing our way forward. Despite what Thorne had said, I'd expected guards, but no doubt they were all at the feast. The Fiend really was complacent. Here at the seat of his power he feared no attack.

The Piper gestured that we should take the lead. Once again, he took up a position behind us.

We walked the length of the passageway, no more than fifty rapid steps, and paused before the huge double doors that blocked our further progress. Beyond it we could hear shouting and merriment – the excited whoops and cries of a raucous rabble gathered for a celebratory feast.

Behind us the Piper suddenly began to play his flute. I had previously thought his tune far different from that of Pan. And, yes, it certainly did differ but there were also similarities. I had a feeling that if those tunes were ever played together, Pan and the Piper standing side by side, they would actually be in harmony.

'Sword!' I commanded and I heard it rasp into the scabbard on my back. There was another rasp as I drew it. I paused, gripping the sword two-handed.

'I think you should knock to beg admittance,' Thorne advised with a grin, drawing two blades of her own. 'A very polite knock is called for!'

I grinned back, understanding exactly what she meant.

My polite left boot struck the doors hard and they burst open, banging back upon the walls.

The babble of conversation halted and there was a sudden silence. It lasted one second at the most as all eyes turned towards us.

Then we attacked.

The layout of the large chamber was exactly as we had been advised and was perfect for three attackers. A trident of tables faced us, ending at the far end of the long room where they joined their base, a longer and higher table with the gigantic horned form of the bestial Fiend seated at its centre.

The other occupants of the four tables were varied in their roughly human appearance but most had the unmistakable lizard scales of demonic entities. They were garbed in leather armour and had weapons too – mostly blades of different sizes and shapes. In many cases these weapons were in sheaths and scabbards upon their monstrous bodies, but a few had laid them on the table alongside their plates.

In that very brief pause before they responded to our intrusion, I wondered about that. The attack would have come as a complete surprise to them, so why the weapons at the ready? It struck me then how Hell was always divided and in constant violent turmoil. The weapons were a precaution against threats from their companions, not an attack from beyond.

I noted the plates heaped high with raw meat dripping blood and the goblets brimming with that same red viscous liquid. No meal for gourmets – this was for cannibal gluttons, a gory feast of blood, flesh and bone.

Then the three of us leaped up onto the tables and began to run towards the Fiend, scattering dishes and slaying demons with each step. First blood went to Thorne who, with her second step upon the tabletop, kicked a wide slim metal dish straight at the throat of a demon to her left. It all but sliced the head from the body.

On my right, Grimalkin was almost dancing as she moved swiftly forward, plucking throwing blades from the straps which criss-crossed her body, and casting them with unerring accuracy at her selected victims as they clambered to their feet and reached towards us. Why one demon was slain while another was passed over I could only guess. No doubt she slew the strongest of the horde, the ones presenting the greater threats.

I used my weapon one-handed, chopping away threats on either side, flicking the sword from hand to hand as it proved necessary while not once reducing the speed of my progress.

We'd covered almost half the length of the room before we first encountered serious opposition. Some of our enemies had clambered up onto the tables and more were doing so with every second that passed. All too soon, as we fought our way forward, our progress slowed considerably. I cut and thrust, driving my opponents back with my sword, but each small advance was the result of a great effort as I felt the resistance of our opponents ahead, too many now moving between us and our target, the Fiend.

For the first time since entering the fortress, I feared failure and doubts assailed me. A voice shrieked inside my head, telling me how ridiculous it was to think that so few of us could triumph against such formidable opposition.

But then I felt something with sharp claws run up my left leg and continue up my back where it halted briefly upon my left shoulder. Out of the corner of my eye, I saw that it was a huge rat. It leaped from my shoulder straight at the demon that I was fighting to overcome. Its jaws fastened upon him and he fell backwards as blood blossomed from his throat.

The music of the Piper was louder now. A huge pack of rats had now followed us onto the tables. They squealed in their eagerness to feed, squirming between our legs or using our upper bodies to launch themselves at our enemies. Grey tails twitched, claws gripped and teeth tore as the demons fell back under their furious onslaught.

Once more we were running, every step taking us closer to the Fiend. I could see him ahead of me now. He had risen to his feet, a huge figure several times the height of a human, his twin coils of ram's horns crowning his ferocious appearance. Our eyes locked and he snarled at me.

But then he was lost to my sight as, once again, more demons moved into position between us. These opponents were larger and succumbed to the rats less easily. They had to be an elite that guarded the Fiend, his personal bodyguards skilled in the arts of combat.

Some of the rats were cut from the air or speared upon dagger-tips. Our progress slowed again and I found myself confronted by a fearsome demon who had more than a hint of an abhuman in his appearance, twin tusks sprouting from beneath his nose and a cavernous mouth over-filled with dagger-like fangs. He was skilled too and matched each stroke of my sword with an effective block. It was several moments before I slew him but immediately another took his place. Once more our attack was being thwarted.

But then the tide of the battle changed again. As I struggled against the next formidable demon who jabbed at me skilfully with a long spear, keeping me at bay and threatening with every thrust to penetrate my guard, he was simply lifted from his feet and yanked upwards towards the high ceiling.

I saw that he was in the grip of a thorny green vine, wick with life, which was coiling and twisting rhythmically as it hauled him towards the ceiling. He was shrieking as he died, being simultaneously strangled and pierced with thorns. More vines were snaking down the walls, finding other victims, while to our rear the Piper continued to play, summoning more rats to replace those already slain.

Depleted, the opposition fell back under our attack and we raced forward again, all three of us reaching the Fiend at about the same time. Grimalkin drew first blood, her blade thrown with accuracy to bury itself deep within the hairy chest. Thorne aimed her own blade at his left eye, but a deft twist of his huge head deflected the blade with his horns. I swung my sword two-handed, my intention being to strike his monstrous head clean from his body. But before my blow landed he changed form.

He changed so rapidly that I was truly astonished.

Using tulpas, I was capable of instantaneously shifting my own shape but I had not been aware that the Fiend also had the skill to do that so quickly. He was reputed to take other forms but I had always thought it a slow and gradual process.

One moment he was human in shape but bestial, hairy and horned with the addition of a long, barbed tail; the next he was a fearsome dragon, with scales as black as ebony, red burning eyes, long murderous fang-filled jaws and sharp talons.

In the first second of his change, he was no larger than he had been previously. But then he flicked his spine-tipped wings and soared aloft, growing rapidly as he rose towards the ceiling. That stone roof did not hinder his ascent. He broke through it and continued into the sky above his redoubt, stones and rubble crashing down into the hall to slay many of his supporters.

Untouched, we stared upwards and I realized what this meant.

He had not fled to escape our attack. He had flown to lure me after him. He wanted to destroy me. This would be his revenge for Churchtown.

I knew I must follow him. I'd be on my own now because although Grimalkin and Thorne could fly in the form of orbs, they could not fight in that shape, the orb being merely a useful method of passing swiftly from one location to another.

'Bring me his thumb-bones!' cried Thorne, grinning wickedly.

'Take care,' said Grimalkin, her face sombre. 'The Fiend is devious and will strike when you least expect it.'

I changed into the sky wolf and flew upwards, aiming for the gaping hole in the ruined ceiling.

29

FANGS AND TEETH

The Fiend struck first. As I emerged into the red baleful glare of Hell's blood moon, I was immediately seconds from death. The Fiend attacked from the direction of that moon, a surge of darkness that eclipsed it as his jaws widened and he savagely snapped his fangs at me.

His dragon shape was immense. Had those fangs made contact, he would have bitten me in half. But somehow, with just inches to spare, I twisted away and soared upwards, just managing to evade a furious swing of his barbed tail.

Now I began to appreciate the enormity of the force ranged against me. If I kept the sky wolf small, I would have great endurance and could probably fly and fight for hours. After all, with neither of us adopting shapes larger than human size, I had fought Circe through a long night and, although steadily weakening, had endured until dawn. But because the Fiend was so large, I must be relatively large too or he might literally swallow me whole.

It was all a question of the energy that I had available. When I'd attacked the Fiend in Churchtown, carried him aloft and impaled him on the spire, my large size meant that I had been capable of just that one attack. Had I missed or been fought off in some way, I would have had to retreat and I would have been helpless, my strength exhausted, as Tom, Alice and Jenny were then sacrificed on the fire.

It had been a gamble that had paid off. But Tilda was right. I was a risk-taker and the sky wolf, which loved combat, was even more reckless than I was.

I realized my own limitations, whereas I had no idea what energy the Fiend had at his disposal. After all, I was now in his domain, Hell. So I had to be cautious and conserve my strength as best I could.

With that in mind, I increased my size to about a third of his and began to climb. He came after me but was still far below. So I stooped, folding my wings, and dropped like a hawk towards its prey, gaining speed with every second.

The Fiend might be powerful and possessed of energy far greater than my own, but could he fight well in the dragon form that he had adopted? I was combat-experienced, first riding thermals and honing my flying skills hunting small creatures for food in the fields and forests of the County. Then I had fought three of Circe's servants who had also taken the shape of dragons. I had slain all three but at a great cost.

Fighting the third, I'd been over-confident, filled with hubris, the sin of pride. Badly wounded, I had only survived and made a full recovery because of the skilful nursing of Tilda and the deployment of her magic.

But I could not afford to rein in the sky wolf too much. I had to allow it to take *some* risks and use its ability to the utmost. So it was that my attack was partly successful.

As I plummeted past my enemy, my talons raked the side of the dragon's neck, slicing through the black scales and drawing blood. I heard the Fiend scream and my confidence soared. But a taloned hand reached towards me and I was lucky to escape.

I had smiled within when the bloodthirsty Thorne had asked me to bring her the Fiend's thumb-bones. I suppose I'd thought it absurd that a dragon should have thumbs. But in the form of the sky wolf I had created hands with taloned fingers but also opposable thumbs so that I could grasp and grip. I now saw that the Fiend had done likewise, and as he had reached towards me I saw that his intention was not to rend me with his outstretched talons. He'd wanted to grip my body and pull me towards him so that he could use his fangs while I was held close.

All too soon I began to feel weary. Was my strength already beginning to ebb? Doubts began to assail me. What chance had I against one of the Old Gods – he who had once been the most powerful of them all? Now, once again, he was in the ascendancy, already having taken control of Hell.

What did I have to counter that? I could take on more than one shape, but I was already within the tulpa that had the best chance against the Fiend. All I truly had was my imagination – my greatest gift that enabled me to visualize tulpas and make those thought-forms take on shape and substance.

How could it help me now?

An extraordinary idea came to me. I could fly straight towards the Fiend and, as his jaws widened, ready to bite and tear my body, I could suddenly become small and fly straight into his huge mouth. Then I could become Black Fang and eat my way up into his brain.

The idea seemed crazy, but was it really that insane?

My reckless self thought that it was the perfect way to win. The other part of me was more cautious. I might not get past the teeth. If I evaded them, he might swallow me whole down into his belly. Then there was my fear of fire . . .

The three dragon-servants of Circe had not breathed fire at me. They had lacked that ability but the Fiend *might* be different. After all, this was Hell where such a thing might easily be possible. I could not risk flying straight towards his jaws.

Then I realized that part of my idea was not that crazy after all. The Fiend was enormous and had grown slowly as he ascended towards the ceiling of the Bone Fortress. But he had not changed size since. Perhaps he couldn't do so? But I *could* do that and could change size very quickly.

So I attacked the Fiend, flying at the same altitude straight at him from the side, aiming to rake the side of his head with my talons. He twisted slowly towards me but, before we were head to head, I shrank in size so that I was no larger than the rabbits that I hunted back in the County. Before he could move his head to seize me in his jaws or twist away to evade me, my own talons cut into his forehead and then sliced through his left eye.

Blinded in that eye, he screamed, and as I soared out of reach he came after me. His greater size gave him the advantage when it came to speed, and as he closed with me a narrow tongue of fire shot from his mouth and passed so close that the hairs on my shoulders and back were singed. So I was right: he could breathe fire.

But I grew again and escaped. I had taken his eye and that would be a great loss. Not only that, his angry reaction to my successful attack had caused him to use fire earlier than he'd doubtlessly intended. Probably he'd been saving it for later if I'd grown complacent, coming to believe that he did not have that ability.

Had I then been taken by surprise, he might have destroyed me. But he'd missed his one chance. Now my wariness would increase.

Our battle seemed timeless. I could not gauge the passing of the minutes and then what became the hours of our aerial conflict. I was hurt again and again: sometimes by searing blasts of fire that were painfully close, other times by talons that raked my body so that blood welled up to streak my hide with red. I particularly feared my wings catching fire, which would cause me to plummet downwards to destruction, leaving a trail of smoke.

But by a mixture of skill and good fortune I avoided the worst of the hurt he intended; and the hurt that I did in return slowly began to take its toll. Many times I tried and failed to take his other eye, which would have ended the battle far earlier. After each failed attack he came after me and each time I barely survived, often swooping low to pass between the tall towers of the Bone Fortress where he could not follow.

Although the passing of time was difficult to judge, I estimate that it was towards the end of the third hour that I first thought that I might win. I had been continuing to tear pieces from him. There were wounds upon his body and holes in his wings. As we fought high above the Bone Fortress, his blood was drizzling down upon its black stones. So I attacked those vulnerable wings with a new fury and resolve, shredding and wounding with each pass, always close to being caught by his fangs. But the more damage I did, the less likely that was to happen.

Finally, his wings became my only target. Those black wings were huge and I began to damage them badly. Some wounds that I inflicted were just small tears and lacerations – but they were cumulative. Then twice I did serious hurt to them, reducing my size to fly straight through the membrane, tearing away some of the structure that enabled flight.

He could no longer use those bloodied wings with the skill he had formerly employed. He could no longer position his head swiftly enough to spit fire with sufficient accuracy to destroy me. He came close a few times, as my singed hide testified, but I was no longer in any serious danger of being engulfed by dragon fire.

At last, the Fiend fell in a long slow spiral, his tattered wings no longer able to support him. He came down close to the Skull Wall, on the level ground immediately before its huge doors, which were still wide open. He hit the ground hard head-first but changed instantly and took on the huge bestial human shape we had confronted at the feast.

But as he staggered to his feet I could see that he was severely damaged, his hairy body streaked with blood and a gaping hole in his left shoulder through which I could glimpse bone. One of his horns had broken off close to his head, reducing it to a stump of bone.

I landed facing the Fiend and I too changed my shape. But I did not take on the form of the warrior.

I became Raphael.

The damage done to one of my bound tulpas affected them all. As Raphael, I was still wracked with the pain of my burns and the injuries to my body inflicted when I was the shape of the sky-wolf. I was losing a lot of blood and it was starting to form a pool beneath my boots. My strength was waning alarmingly but I could still deliver one final blow. But it would need to be perfectly executed.

I cast aside the sword that Raphael carried. I would need a better weapon than that to slay the most powerful of the Old Gods.

'Sword!' I cried, and it appeared in my hands – the deadly magical weapon given to me by the Piper.

I unfurled my wings and rose a couple of feet into the air. I had chosen well in taking on the form of Raphael. What more fitting than that an angel should slay the Devil? Just as, on one level, Piddle believed that he was a small mongrel dog, Raphael truly believed that he was an angel high in Heaven's hierarchy. He was filled with loathing and righteous anger at being confronted by the enemy of all that he served.

Just as I often allowed the sky wolf licence to fight with fury while taking incredible risks, now I gave that same freedom to Raphael. He did not hesitate. He struck one powerful blow with astonishing speed.

We sliced the head of the Fiend clean from his body. It rolled across the stones as the huge bestial body collapsed to its knees, flopped onto its side, twitched once and then became still with true death.

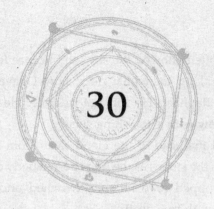

30

NON SERVIAM!

When that task was completed, I became the warrior once more and gazed down at the body of my enemy which now lay upon the ground before me in two pieces.

Grimalkin and Thorne emerged from the dark doorway covered in gore. Thorne ran on ahead towards me.

'May I take his thumb-bones, Wulf?' Thorne cried.

'They are yours if you want them,' I replied, suddenly feeling a great weariness fall upon me and my vision grow dark. Blood was still trickling from my body, the pool beneath my boots growing larger.

'One for you and one for me?' asked Thorne, looking back towards Grimalkin as a daughter might ask permission from her mother.

'They are both yours, child,' said the witch assassin. 'I want nothing from that filthy beast. After having carried his ugly head in a sack for many long months, I never want to be close to any part of him ever again – even his bones.'

Grimalkin's words filled me with anxiety. I remembered *why* she had carried that head. It had been to keep it out of the clutches of the Fiend's servants. They had wished to join it to his body once more so that he could walk the earth. Could he be returned to life so easily?

'What about now? Is there a risk that his servants might reattach his head to his body?' I asked Grimalkin, glancing down at his remains.

As Thorne knelt down, drew a blade and began her grisly task, Grimalkin shook her head.

'I have spoken to the Piper about that,' she said. 'We have planned to ensure that cannot happen.'

No sooner had Thorne risen to her feet grasping her grisly trophies than a horde of rats began to emerge from the doorway. These were larger than any that I had previously seen and they ran directly towards the Fiend.

'Give them room to work!' said Grimalkin. We stepped back and did as she'd commanded.

They began to devour the Fiend, swarming all over him, eating the flesh and crunching the bones with their monstrous teeth. Soon, nothing of him would remain.

'Will this finally be the end of him?' I asked. I could feel my body trembling and felt a strange weakness in my knees. Blood still dripped from me.

Again, Grimalkin shook her head. 'It will be the end of him for quite a while. But as you may know gods depend upon faith and belief for their birth and continued existence. When enough foolish humans and witches wish to call upon the Fiend and serve him, he will eventually respond and return.'

Suddenly the ground seemed to lurch up towards me and I fell to my knees.

I could hear Thorne and Grimalkin talking together but their voices seemed faint and distant and I only heard one word which they repeated more than once . . .

Poison.

Although my wounds were numerous, they were relatively minor, but as I learned later the fangs and talons of the Fiend introduce a deadly poison into the blood of any creature that they wound.

It is a fatal poison.

I lay in a dark room of black stone, lit by a single small torch, where my needs were attended to. I sweated with fever and was mostly unconscious and unaware of those who ministered to me.

I owed my survival primarily to Thorne who became my nurse and rarely left my side. The Piper too played his part and it was his strong magic that sustained me while I hovered between life and death. Finally, he withdrew. Whether he had reached the limits of his power and gave up on me I do not know. But it did not matter because it was then that another intervened.

It was Thorne who told me what happened. A natural spring of water appeared in the rock wall, while herbs began to sprout from the floor of my small room, a forest of furious growth, its tangled roots embedded in the very stones. Those herbs brought the Piper back. It seemed that many of them were unknown to him. They had no names. But apparently a gift from an Old God, it would be safe for me to swallow them – they did not have the same effect as foods from the dark. Quite the opposite, in fact.

So he experimented, boiling, mixing and blending until he finally concocted a mixture that took away the worst of my fever and set my heart beating stronger and more steadily, the healing water adding strength to my dwindling life force. Then it was that the being who had caused the herbs to sprout from the stones, and the water to flow for me, came to visit me.

First could be heard the playing of pipes, a wild music that throbbed in the air and made the very stones vibrate.

The boy with curly hair and pointy ears did not manifest himself but I heard the voice of Pan whispering in my ear while a small black cat sat upon my chest and purred loudly.

'Will you serve me?' he asked.

Weak as I was, I shook my head. 'I thank you for saving my life, but I serve nobody,' I told him.

'I will ask you again,' said the voice of Pan. 'Will you serve me?'

'I serve nobody,' I said and the cat ceased its purring.

'One final time I will ask!' The voice of Pan hissed like a snake. 'Will you serve me?'

I thought it foolish to serve a god. I remembered poor Alice and all the difficulties that it had caused her – once even separating her from Tom, the one she loved. I was also weary beyond the point of caring and beyond fear.

And I was angry. Who were these gods to manipulate humans and meddle in our affairs? We were better left alone to make our own mistakes. Thus, my third reply was calculated and intended to anger Pan and I did not care. I just wished to be left alone. I remembered a sermon that the Abbot had preached to the monks. He told how the Devil had defied God and rejected him. The words that the Devil had spoken were in Latin. That was my final answer to Pan: another reckless repetition of what I had already said.

'*Non serviam!*' I cried.

I thought that Pan would become angry at that reply and either destroy me or leave, but the voice that continued to whisper in my ears was calm.

'You serve me just by being who you are!' he said.

Suddenly my room was filled with creatures both large and small. Butterflies and moths filled the air above my sickbed and the cat began to purr again.

We continued to talk and gradually my attitude began to soften. I remember agreeing to certain things that he suggested because they served both our interests. But later, when I recovered, I couldn't remember what he'd asked and what I'd promised. It all seemed too much like a dream.

When Pan finally left my side, I was healed. I was weak but the Piper assured me that I would recover. They left it to Thorne to tell me the really bad news.

'It was difficult to heal you, even for Pan,' she said, smiling at me but with a hint of sadness round her eyes. 'It took a lot of time. Much more time than you will have realized. I am afraid . . . you will never see Tilda again,' she told me.

My heart lurched and a wave of terrible sadness threatened to overwhelm me. 'What do you mean? Have I stayed here too long? Can't I leave? May I never return to earth?'

Thorne smiled at me sadly. 'You can go back, Wulf. But you have been away so long that everybody you knew on earth will now be dead.'

I had known that as far as time was concerned, Hell sometimes behaved in a similar fashion to that of an underworld such as Hrothgar's. Sometimes time moved at the same rate as it did on earth. At other times it could be far different. Thorne now explained to me how the cause of that was often an event of significance. The slaying of Circe had disturbed time here but with a relatively small consequence. The destruction of the Fiend, the ruler of Hell, had brought about a much larger effect.

At least a century had passed on earth.

And my action in defeating the Fiend had brought that about.

I was the author of my own anguish.

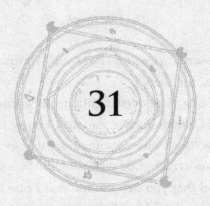

31

A Hunter of the Dark

As I walked towards the door with Thorne, I was overcome by a great sadness. I knew already what to expect beyond it. There was no hope. Everyone I had known, including Tilda, would be gone. Although I'd had a little time to reconcile myself to that, the pain of my loss had suddenly returned stronger than ever.

Then I had a sudden shock that momentarily took away my breath. Thorne slipped her hand into mine and squeezed. Her hand was very cold. I tried not to flinch but one glance at her told me that she was aware of my reaction. She looked hurt.

'You're rejecting me because I'm dead!' Thorne said bitterly.

'No, I don't,' I protested. 'When you held my hand suddenly like that, it was a shock – that's all.'

'Don't I deserve to love and be loved?' Thorne demanded.

'Of course,' I replied.

'I died young. I enjoyed fighting our enemies and the training that Grimalkin gave me. And I enjoy fighting here with her now. But I missed something that everyone born upon earth has a right to. So why should it be a shock, Wulf? Don't pretend that you don't know that I care for you. I've done everything I could to let you know that – everything but speak it aloud, and now I'm doing just that. I know that I can never replace Tilda but I can be a comfort to you. We can comfort each other. Why be alone?'

I stared at her, searching for something to say. I uttered the first words that came into my head. 'Where are the bones of the Fiend that you were so eager to take?' I asked.

She shrugged, her face full of disappointment – no doubt because I'd changed the subject. 'They are too large to wear!' she said. 'Worn on my necklace they would reach down almost to my waist! But Grimalkin and I have kept them somewhere safe. They are full of powerful magic and if it ever proves necessary we shall use it.'

We halted at the door and Thorne stared at me hard.

'One day you will need me,' she said softly. 'Call my name and I will come to your side. Will you do that?'

'If I need you, yes, I will call your name,' I told her.

It wasn't a lie but I knew it was probably never going to happen. I felt sorry for her and knew that, despite her friendship with Grimalkin, she was lonely. But at that moment all I could think of was my own loss. Being back in Hrothgar's underworld and in his dwelling where Tilda and I had spent so much time together would be hard to bear.

I looked over my shoulder and took one final glance at the blood moon. The last thing I saw in Hell was Thorne's sad face. I smiled at Thorne, then I opened the door and left it all behind.

As the door closed behind me, I stood perfectly still and listened carefully. The torches ignited with a *whoosh* and then gave out their usual flickering yellow light but I looked to my right and saw that the cages were empty. Probably the tulpas had been destroyed – Alice and Tom would have thought it the best thing to do before leaving the underworld.

No doubt Tilda would have agreed with that. They would have waited a long time for me – especially Tilda. But you can't wait forever. I had been away far too long. Now they would all be gone, passed from the earth to somewhere else.

I walked as far as the second door and became Saint Quentin. It opened easily. I remembered how it had defied me previously. No doubt Alice had attended to that also. Her magic would recognize me. I would be the exception to the normal rule. When I stepped through and closed it behind me, the original magical lock would probably engage again. Alice would have thought of that. Only I would be permitted through. It would remain sealed against any future danger from the dark.

As if to confirm that, the moment I stepped through the third and final door into Hrothgar's mansion, it slammed shut behind me and I could hear strange noises from within it as if the full locking mechanism with all its attendant magic was now fully engaging once more.

And after that there was silence. The silence of an empty dwelling.

The first shock was Hrothgar's library. It had been looted, the books stolen from the shelves. I felt a wrench at that, a strong sense of loss. I could have learned a lot about my craft from those books. My only hope was that Tom Ward might have taken some of them to add to the library at Chipenden.

The vandalism was widespread. Ladders had been torn from the walls, the tables and chairs broken. A cold draught filled the library also – some of the windows had gone, leaving holes for the whistling wind, while others were cracked.

The rest of the house was in the same state: more smashed windows, furniture broken, wood scattered on the floor and, in those facing west, pools of water or damp on the floors.

The next major shock was waiting for me outside. The red baleful sky was no more. It had been replaced by dark grey clouds driven by a cold blustering westerly wind. I could distinctly smell rain upon that chill wind.

With the death of Hrothgar, his underworld had collapsed and vanished. The house and grounds were now part of the County. I glanced at the trees in the distance, the perimeter wood once inhabited by Hrothgar's monstrous guardian tulpas. Most had lost their leaves – it was late autumn and, judging by the cold edge to the wind, winter wasn't very far away.

I felt weary. My strength was far from fully returned and now back in the world I was all too aware of my weakness. I went back into the abandoned house and curled up in a corner of the library and slept. When I awoke it was dark. I was hungry so I took the shape of the sky wolf and went hunting.

I flew over the village and was dismayed to see how much it had grown again. It confirmed what Thorne had told me – too many years had elapsed for me to have any real hope of finding Tilda and her parents still alive. I could have flown north to Chipenden but I didn't want that bleak confirmation of what I knew in my heart was true.

On my return to the empty mansion, I slept again. I couldn't bear to be awake. My sense of loss was too great.

Then, soon after dawn, one of the wolf tulpas returned. It was Bone. I was astonished by that, expecting that my absence beyond the doors would have caused the gristles to disintegrate and fall back into heaps of bone dust and dry clay. All I could think was that the drops of Tilda's blood

293

added in the process of their creation had allowed them to endure.

I patted the grey fur of the beast and my spirits lifted a little. I was no longer alone.

Within three days, all six of them had returned and were sharing the shelter of the library with me. By then I had taken on the shape of the wolf called Black Fang. We hunted together but gradually moved north and left the County far behind. Then we journeyed even further and entered another country of high hills and bleak moors. As the winter advanced, the snow gripped the land and prey became harder to find. In this northern land we encountered other wolves too and their blood reddened the snow. They were food too.

For a while I became so immersed in living the life of Black Fang that I forgot that I was also human. My thoughts and much of my memory fled. But perhaps the truth was that I did not want the pain of my memories. I got my wish and all that remained was the feelings and instincts of a beast. But, despite the adversity we faced, I grew stronger with each month that passed.

As the winter moved towards its end we drifted south again and once more I found myself in the County and my mind gradually began to sharpen and a few memories slowly returned. I led us to the Chipenden house and we circled the garden, keeping our distance because I could sense the threat within, the dangerous boggart that still roamed the perimeter.

Dimly, deep within me, more memories of that house awoke. I knew that nothing much would have changed. Despite the passage of many years, nobody would have dared to enter that garden.

I lacked the wit to transform myself back into the human tulpa that the boggart would recognize and allow entry. But my sense of smell told me that the house was deserted. No humans had visited for many years. At the time I couldn't remember who those people were, but deep within me there was a sense of sadness, a feeling of something lost that could never be recovered.

At last, as the weather mellowed, we returned to Hrothgar's mansion and spent the first few weeks of spring using the library as our shelter once more. But then, awakening suddenly from a dream of hunting and the pleasure of my teeth fastening upon the throat of my prey, a sudden memory returned to me. It was a clear remembrance of how this room had once been, its shelves lined with books and the ceiling very high to accommodate the dimensions of a tall thin giant.

There was something else that, at first, I struggled to remember. There had been a stout stick leaning against the library wall and there was something important about it. It did not belong to me but I had once borrowed it for a while.

No, it was not just a stick. It was called a *staff*.

It had been made out of rowan wood, something that was very effective against creatures of the dark, especially witches.

The staff had belonged to a spook called Tom Ward.

Within days, I was wandering the house and grounds in human shape, while my pack of grey wolves stared at me and occasionally whined softly. They sensed that something had changed. They preferred things the way they had been.

If I had not battled the Fiend in Hell, I could have studied at Hrothgar's mansion for years, safe within his underworld. I could have honed my skills and deepened my knowledge. But that was no longer possible. I realized that I was destined to become something different from the tulpar who had taught me. Hrothgar had been something of a scholar and to increase his knowledge had been his primary aim.

My goal was different.

Like Tom Ward before me, I would become a hunter of the dark.

I would be the last Spook.

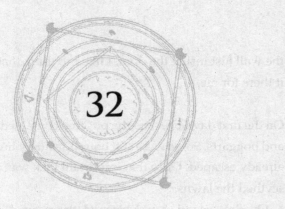

32

THE TRAP

Late in the spring, I sent my pack of wolves away. But they knew that I would summon them when the need arose. In the shape of the warrior, I strode north towards Chipenden, delighting in the feel of the breeze upon my face and the warmth of the sun on my head and shoulders.

The boggart gave a low growl as I entered the garden. Then it whined and withdrew. It knew who I was. It knew that I belonged here. The garden was overgrown, the grass already knee-high with tall saplings shooting up everywhere.

The house was securely locked but, as I had anticipated, abandoned. This time I did not hesitate in entering. A lot of work needed to be done. Although there was nobody there to welcome me back, Tom Ward's staff was leaning against the wall just inside the door. I liked to think that he had left it there for me.

On the first day, I checked the pits that contained the witches and boggarts. Some were still bound securely but others had already escaped. Once that important task was dealt with, I scythed the lawns.

On the second day, I cleaned the ground floor of the Chipenden house, dusting and sweeping, then washing and wiping pots, pans and plates. I also threw out what was beyond repair.

On the third day, I dealt with the library. Some of the books were full of mildew or rotted and beyond saving. Those I burned, making a large bonfire in the garden. I enjoyed watching the sparks fly up into the sky. I was sorry for the loss of the books, but a good fire always cheers me up. And there were still plenty of books left, and among them I was delighted to find many that dealt with the craft of creating tulpas. Tom Ward had always known the worth of books. He must have taken the best of Hrothgar's library and added them to the Chipenden legacy.

And in the library there was something new. A great clock that Tom or Alice must have added to the furniture. It was what was sometimes called a *grandfather clock* with a tall casing below the clockface which housed a pendulum. The clock had stopped but I set that pendulum swinging again and soon the *tick-tock* of the clock resounded like the steady beat of a new heart.

On the fourth day, I cleaned the upper floors, taking special care with the small bedroom that was traditionally used by the Spook's apprentices. I liked the way the names were written on the wall – over thirty of them who'd been trained in this house.

There were other larger bedrooms, but this was my favourite – the place where I had first stayed when I had met Tom Ward and later when I had visited here with Tilda. It reminded me of happier times. This was where I intended to sleep.

On the fifth day, I repaired the bell at the withy trees crossroads. Then, carrying my staff and a hessian sack, I strolled down into the village and visited the butchers, buying bacon and pork chops. I walked around for a while calling at other shops, purchasing bread and cheese and vegetables while making sure that folks knew that a new spook was now working from the house.

On the sixth day, I visited the graves. The new ones were there as I had predicted, all close to the seat where spooks trained their apprentices, weather permitting.

I started with the grave of John Gregory and then dealt with the larger one where I saw Tom and Alice were buried together. I smiled. They would like that, even if they may not be together in the afterlife, Tom heading for the light while Alice went to the dark. Tilda had once confided in me that her mother's greatest fear was that they would be separated after death. So there was a mystery here too. If Alice had truly gone to the dark, wouldn't I have seen her before I left that grim place?

Beyond that double grave was a smaller one for Tilda. I couldn't look at that one too long. Then I saw there was no grave for Jenny. I assumed that once she'd grown old, she'd gone off to spend her final days elsewhere. I wondered what had happened. After Tom and Alice had died had Jenny become the local spook for a while? If she had died, might she come back yet again? As one of the Samhadre, she seemed to have the power to do so. One day I hoped to find out.

Despite my intention to be strong, I wept at the loss of my friends. Then I cut the surrounding grass neatly and scraped and scrubbed the stones so that the inscriptions could be read clearly.

On the seventh day, I went fishing. I walked down to the River Hodder and after a bit of experimenting with my bait I finally managed to catch a couple of trout. I gave each of them back to Pan and they swam away vigorously.

On the eighth day, the bell rang at the withy trees, summoning me to Spook's business. I found an old man waiting there who asked me to sort out a bone witch who'd taken up residence in Coot's Valley Farm, which had been abandoned years earlier. She'd been begging locally and cursing anyone who refused to give. He said that three children had died already. Yesterday, one of the graves had been robbed of its bones.

He paid me in advance, claiming to have collected the money from terrified locals.

I ignored the sly look in his piggy eyes.

It was just less than an hour's walk to my destination, so I set off before eleven, planning to arrive before midnight. I wasn't carrying my staff or bag. After about twenty minutes or so someone stepped out of the trees and approached me.

It was a young priest, hardly older than I'd been on leaving the abbey for the final time.

'I've come to ask you a favour,' he said. 'My church is being plagued by a troublesome boggart. It rattles the gate and throws stones onto the roof. Most of my flock are too afraid to attend services. It's Saint Mary's and not that far from here . . .'

I was surprised to be asked for such help by a priest but I smiled at him and nodded. 'I'll deal with it just as soon as I can,' I told him, preparing to move on.

'I would like you to come now,' he insisted. 'It's most important that you do so!'

I shook my head. 'I have my own urgent business to attend to right now. The boggart will still be there tomorrow.'

At that, he stepped forward and gripped my sleeve, his hand trembling. I glared at him until he released me. 'If I cannot lead you to safety elsewhere then I can at least warn you,' he said. 'Hell is gathering in Coot's Valley. Led by a monstrous devil with three eyes, a horde of demons and witches has travelled from miles around to congregate there! They are there waiting for *you*. Don't go there. You are being lured into a trap.'

I was pleased to receive his warning. Most priests wouldn't even lift a finger to aid a spook.

'Thank you for the warning, Father,' I told him, 'but please don't worry about me. Pray for your flock and for yourself and I'll deal with your boggart tomorrow at dusk.'

I walked on into the darkness. Alone and feeling the need for a little company, I summoned my grey wolves: Tooth, Claw, Blood, Bone, Hide and Hair.

They bounded towards me out of the darkness and I fell to my knees and patted them in turn. I could tell that they were really hungry. I walked on and they took up their usual positions, three on my right and three on my left. The saliva from their open jaws glistened in the moonlight as it dripped onto the grass.

I had almost reached the lip of the valley now and my heart started to beat faster with anticipation and excitement.

There was a faint sound then, carried upon the breeze. It brought the wolves to a sudden halt, their ears flattening backwards. They were listening to that distant music.

Pan was playing his pipes.

Pausing to listen, I remembered something of our conversation.

'Seeds!' I cried.

Suddenly my mouth filled with bitter seeds and I spat them onto the ground directly in front of me. Then I used my imagination. Inspiration came on wings and I pointed their potential towards precisely what I wanted.

Within moments thorny verdant vines erupted from the earth and began to race left and right like green fire to encircle the valley. They would soon form an impenetrable barrier with only one entrance, which was directly ahead of me.

'Sword!' I commanded, and there was a pleasing rasp as it inserted itself into the empty scabbard upon my back. There was a louder rasp as I reached over my left shoulder and drew it, gripping it firmly with two hands.

Then I gave a third command:

'Thorne!'

Immediately, a silver orb floated down towards me and quickly became a grinning girl bristling with blades.

The young priest had been right.

Yes, it was a trap.

But it was *my* trap.

Join Wulf on more of his
amazing adventures!

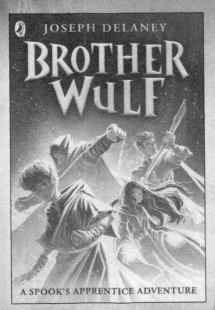

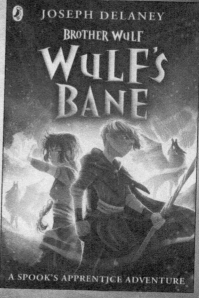

THE SPOOK'S SERIES

WARNING:
NOT TO BE READ AFTER DARK

READ MORE OF JOSEPH DELANEY'S SPOOKY SERIES!

Crafty can't remember a time before the Shole –
a terrifying mist that will either kill you or
transform you into a terrifying monster,
known as an aberration. When Crafty is
recruited to join the Castle in the fight against
this evil, his life is changed forever . . .

JOSEPH DELANEY used to be an English teacher, before becoming the best-selling author of the Spook's series, which has been translated into thirty languages and sold millions of copies. The first book, *The Spook's Apprentice*, was made into a major motion picture starring Jeff Bridges and Julianne Moore.

IF YOU'D LIKE TO LEARN MORE ABOUT JOSEPH AND HIS BOOKS, VISIT:

www.josephdelaneyauthor.com

www.penguin.co.uk